If Only You Knew

A Hotlanta Novel

TML

Also by Denene Millner and Mitzi Miller

Hotlanta

(With Angela Burt-Murray)

The Angry Black Woman's Guide to Life

The Vow

Also by Denene Millner

The Sistahs' Rules:
Secrets for Meeting, Getting, and
Keeping a Good Black Man

Dreamgirls

Also by Denene Millner
(with Nick Chiles)

What Brothers Think, What Sistahs Know

What Brothers Think, What Sistahs Know about Sex:
The Real Deal on Passion, Loving, and Intimacy

Money, Power, Respect:
What Brothers Think, What Sistahs Know

Love Don't Live Here Anymore

In Love & War

A Love Story

If Only You Knew

A Hotlanta Novel

Denene Millner
Mitzi Miller

Point

Trademarks used herein are owned by their respective trademark owners and are used without permission.

If you purchased this book without a cover, you should be aware that this book is stolen property. It was reported as "unsold and destroyed" to the publisher, and neither the author nor the publisher has received any payment for this "stripped book."

 Published by POINT, an imprint of Scholastic Inc., *Publishers since 1920.* SCHOLASTIC, POINT, and associated logos are trademarks and/or registered trademarks of Scholastic Inc.

Library of Congress Cataloging-in-Publication Data
Millner, Denene.
If only you knew : a Hotlanta novel / Denene Millner [and] Mitzi Miller. — 1st ed.
p. cm. — (Hotlanta)
Summary: Wealthy and beautiful African American twins Sydney and Lauren both face boyfriend problems as they continue to delve into a murder mystery that somehow involves both their father and stepfather.
ISBN-13: 978-0-545-00309-4
ISBN-10: 0-545-00309-1
[1. Sisters — Fiction. 2. Twins — Fiction. 3. Fathers and daughters — Fiction. 4. Stepfathers — Fiction. 5. Schools — Fiction. 6. Wealth — Fiction. 7. African Americans — Fiction. 8. Atlanta (Ga.) — Fiction.] I. Miller, Mitzi. II. Title.
PZ7.M63957If 2008
[Fic] — dc22 2007050723

12 11 10 9 8 7 6 5 4 3 2 1

Printed in the U.S.A.
First edition, October 2008
Book design by Steve Scott. Text set in Bulmer, Peignot, and Delta Jaeger.

For the beautiful boys who will grow up to be the men of our dreams.

Mazi Chiles —
A Northern gentleman with Southern charm poised
to make his mark on the world . . .
— D.M.

John Aden Harvey —
My genius godson who never stops
coming back for more . . .
— M.M.

1
SYDNEY

"Five, four, three, two," Sydney Duke muttered under her breath as the last seconds of AP Global History slowly ticked away. The bell barely sounded before she and her new brown crocodile Bottega Veneta shoulder bag were halfway to the door. After the last class of the day on a Friday, Sydney was more than ready to leave the Korean War to the few remaining veterans and get the heck up out of Dodge. Not to mention, since the huge Thanksgiving holiday party she and her twin sister were planning at the family's Lake Lanier vacation house was exactly a month away, she and her best friends had some serious dress shopping to get into at Phipps Plaza.

"Um, may I have a word with you please, Miss Duke?" Her teacher's rhetorical question brought Sydney's attempted escape to a screeching halt.

"Yes, ma'am," Sydney responded automatically as she covered the involuntary cringe with her best fake smile before turning around.

"I just wanted to make sure that everything was okay," the well-dressed historian started as the last of Sydney's classmates headed eagerly out the door. "You've seemed a little, um, distracted in class this week."

Considering the love of her life had just played her out by cheating with her twin sister's scandalous former best friend, Dara, Sydney found her instructor's word choice a tad ironic. "No, Dr. Pitts, everything is just fine," she replied, unconsciously twisting the diamond stud in her right ear.

"Oh, okay, 'cause I heard that you and Marcus were no longer . . ."

For a brief moment, Sydney was sure a hole would open up in the floor and swallow her alive. It was bad enough that the entire student body couldn't stop gossiping about the huge blow-up at the Homecoming Benefit Gala where the mild mannered (and *extremely* appearance conscious) school sweetheart, Sydney Duke, flipped out and at the top of her lungs basically told Brookhaven's infallible golden boy, Marcus Green, to kiss her butt. But now the faculty was up in the mix, too? If she wasn't before, Sydney Duke was now officially tapped out.

"Ev-, ev-, everything is just fine," Sydney stuttered,

unsure of how to proceed. Not that she would ever discuss her feelings of insecurity with a teacher — or anyone else if she could help it — but Sydney was far from fine.

Together, Marcus and Sydney had formed Brookhaven's most formidable "it" couple in years. Nicknamed "The Black Ken & Barbie" by peers, parents and apparently even teachers were huge supporters of the four-year relationship. Add to the equation an extremely wealthy family, outstanding academic achievement, and nonstop community service, and Sydney's status on the list of Brookhaven's most influential students seemed almost untouchable. However, lately life was feeling far less insulated.

"Okay, dear," the well-meaning older woman continued, seemingly unaware of the rising blush in Sydney's normally caramel-colored cheeks. "Well, if you ever need someone to talk to, I'm here. Have a good weekend."

"You do the same, ma'am," Sydney offered through clenched teeth as she made a mental note to fling herself off the nearest bridge, then turned on her heel and finally exited the room.

"And just what are the two of you over here whispering about, huh? How to hack into Mr. Kirkland's computer files before finals?" Sydney Duke jokingly asked Carmen and Rhea as she walked up behind the two girls leaning against a white Lexus GS in the middle of the Brookhaven student parking lot.

"Hey, Syd!" Carmen exclaimed turning around to give her BFF a quick kiss on the cheek. "Love the bag . . ." As the only child of extremely wealthy older parents, Carmen had taste like Sydney's — it always leaned a little toward the conservative but extremely expensive.

"Gracias," Sydney responded.

"Girl, please. I need to figure out how to get into those files —" the most outspoken of the three girls, Rhea, huffed as she pulled her shoulder-length hair up into a loose ponytail at the top of her head and fussed with her bangs. "I'm sure every student in Brookhaven would thank me."

"Mm-hmm, and I'm sure you'd be the most popular prisoner down in Fulton County," Sydney assured Rhea as she carefully placed her bag on the car's hood and surveyed the crowded parking lot where at least half of the student body milled about, giving good-bye hugs and making plans for later.

"Whatever," Rhea continued as she now dug in the bottom of her oversized silver Cole Haan bag for her car keys. "If it's between going to jail and telling my parents that I failed freaking health class, I'd rather go to jail!"

"Um, I hear ya, Foxy Brown," Carmen teased good-naturedly. "Just don't call my house collect in the middle of the night crying about your cellmate named Big Bertha.

'Cause you know poor Harold and Anita's nerves be bad. And, I don't want to be an orphan before I turn eighteen."

"Why are you so retarded?" Rhea asked as all three girls burst into laughter. Carmen and Sydney exchanged high fives and finger snaps.

"Wow, it's so beautiful out today," Sydney sighed when she finally caught her breath. "I can't believe it's this warm in November." She stretched her arms overhead to try and relieve some of the tension from her conversation with Dr. Pitts.

"I know that's right," Rhea co-signed as she triumphantly pulled her keys out of the bottom of her bag. With a click of a button, all the windows automatically lowered. She tossed her bag onto the driver's seat and settled back against the car.

"Seems like nobody wants to go home," Carmen commented as she surveyed the faces of some of Atlanta's most privileged African-American kids from behind her favorite pair of oversized Tom Ford sunglasses. "Considering how folks ran out of last period like the roof was on fire . . ."

"Speaking of which, what took you so long to get out here, Syd?" Rhea asked as she closed her eyes and turned her face up to the warm three o'clock sun.

Sydney paused. Even though she loved Carmen and Rhea as much as, if not more than, her outrageous and often infuriating drama queen twin, Lauren — it was still hard to admit when life wasn't going as planned. Which is why, even after all these years, neither Carmen nor Rhea knew the truth about Sydney's biological father, Dice Jackson — the career felon with a gun-smuggling record. Not that Sydney was in denial. But, as she rationalized every time she snuck over to her Aunt Lorraine's house on a side of town neither Carmen nor Rhea would imagine Sydney even knew existed to pick up one of his letters from lockdown, some secrets were best kept hidden.

Applying the same train of thought, Sydney had never discussed any of her suspicions about Marcus cheating until after things hit the fan at the Gala. And even then, it took days and a whole lot of humble pie before she was able to come totally clean about how her once rock-solid relationship completely disintegrated. Thankfully, like true friends, neither passed judgment on Sydney. Instead they became her most ardent supporters.

"You wouldn't believe me if I told you," she finally sighed.

"Good grief, what now?" Carmen asked adamantly. As Sydney and Marcus's breakup continued to be the hot topic all over school as well as online at YoungRichandTriflin.com, the infamous blog created by an anonymous Brookhaven student and dedicated solely to the behind-the-scenes rumors, gossip, and scandal at the prestigious private school, the girls had become accustomed to hearing more and more outrageous "theories" for the couple's split each day. "Did you discover he had a second row of teeth in his head?"

"Almost," Sydney smiled slightly. "Dr. Pitts asked to speak to me after class —"

"For what," Rhea cut Sydney off with a roll of the eyes. Ever since Dr. Pitts had issued Rhea an after-school detention for sending text messages during class, she was officially on the least favorite teacher of all time list.

"Wait on it." Sydney drew the hard pause for effect and continued sarcastically, "She wanted to know if I was okay. Apparently she, too, has heard about the breakup. Can you believe that?"

"What?" Carmen yelped as her jaw dropped open.

"See, I knew I didn't like that nosy old lady!" Rhea started shaking her ponytail furiously and muttering, "Asking a million unnecessary questions, giving folks detention for sending one stupid text message, man, listen."

"Like seriously, I was so mortified," Sydney said somberly as she picked at a spot on her olive-colored Stella jeans.

"I'm sorry, Syd," Carm offered, reaching out to touch Sydney's arm as the hurt streaked across her best friend's face. "That's horrible. I can't even imagine."

Sydney inhaled deeply and forced a smile on her face. "What are you gonna do, huh? Like I always say, keep it moving."

"Mmm-hmm, speak of the devil," Rhea stated cryptically as she locked her sights on three approaching figures. Sydney followed the line of vision across the parking lot to Marcus and two female classmates who were laughing just a little too hard at whatever was being said.

"You've got to be kidding me," Carmen said as she stood straight up and scowled protectively.

"Is he serious? Caroline Morrison? Trina Beddleman? Those girls can't even string a sentence together without help from Hooked on Phonics," Rhea continued as the trio steadily approached.

"Hey, hey, hey, guys, play nice," Sydney said, half-heartedly trying to calm her girls down. Contrary to what had occurred at the Gala, Sydney Duke generally prided herself on behaving like a lady at all times. And that included both a strict no gossiping in public policy, as well as resisting the burning urge to rip every last piece of tacky weave out of Caroline's and Trina's heads for blatantly pushing up on Marcus.

In preparation for the inevitable confrontation, Sydney turned slightly so that Rhea and Carmen could give her outfit a quick once-over. No sooner had they given discreet nods of approval than Marcus and crew were standing on either side of the silver Lincoln Navigator parked directly in front of the girls.

"Hey, y'all," Caroline and Trina called out in sugary voices as Trina clicked the remote access for the locks.

"Hey," Rhea and Carmen offered lamely as Sydney simply smiled coldly and waved with a limp wrist. Picking up the not so subliminal "you're playing yourself" message loud and clear, both girls got into the SUV and started the engine.

"What's up, ladies," Marcus called out as he stopped to pull his dreadlocks back from his chiseled face before opening the front passenger door.

"What's up with *you*," Rhea answered pointedly, while Carmen simply shrugged her greeting and turned away dismissively. Sydney just looked at him blankly.

"Chilling," he continued with the same engaging smile that just weeks ago would have melted Sydney's heart to a puddle. "So what, y'all waiting on Syd's new football homeboy to get out of practice or something?" he asked snidely, referring to star player, co-captain of Brookhaven's varsity football team, and all-round cutie Jason Danden. Sydney and Jason had spontaneously developed a casual friendship in the weeks leading up to the breakup that unfortunately got caught directly in the crosshairs at the Homecoming Benefit Gala. Since that ill-fated night, Sydney had been way too embarrassed to speak to Jason again. But as far as she was concerned, Marcus didn't need to know that.

"Wouldn't you like to know," Sydney countered without flinching.

"Do you, Sydney," Marcus retorted as he jumped in the truck and slammed the door. With a single beep, Trina sped out of the parking lot.

"Are you okay?" Carmen asked hesitantly as soon as the SUV was out of sight.

Sydney looked down at the pavement and started twisting her right earring again. "Sure, I mean . . . it's not like . . ."

"Whatever, girl, forget Marcus. I swear, he's the worst," Rhea rallied as she opened the driver's side door and got inside. "His stock is totally downgraded as far as I'm concerned."

"You think?" Sydney questioned quietly without looking up. " 'Cause clearly every girl in this school seems more than happy to be all up in his face now that I'm not around. Maybe I made a —"

"They're scavengers," Rhea countered.

"Absolutely," Carmen agreed emphatically as she followed Rhea's lead and opened the car's back door to get in. "Like even if we didn't know about sloppy 'ole Dara, Caroline Morrison is so not you. Even on your worst day . . ."

"Not even on a dare," Rhea said with fierce conviction as she slipped on her black Gucci aviators and pulled down the visor to admire her reflection. Satisfied, she turned to Sydney.

"Now will you please get your cute butt in this car so we can go shopping?"

" 'Cause you know, Miss Duke," Carmen continued with a grin, "Mama needs some new shoes to *what*?"

Confidence restored, Sydney looked up at her waiting girlfriends with a huge smile on her face. "Keep. It. *Moving*."

When Rhea finally pulled around the fountain in front of the Duke's Buckhead estate five hours later, Sydney carried six huge shopping bags full of new items and a much-improved outlook on life. "I'll hit you guys tomorrow afternoon when I get home from volunteering," she promised, holding the door open for Carmen to hop in the front. "Maybe we can pass by that barbeque at Tracee's house. I heard her saying that her parents were having it completely catered 'cause her maid quit."

"That's funny. But knowing Tracee's crazy mama, I believe it," Rhea replied as she sipped the last of her strawberry smoothie. "I actually have a twelve-thirty to get my ends cut, but I should be done by the time you finish at the shelter."

"I'm supposed to meet Michael at the shop during his lunch break, but that's not definite," Carmen offered as she closed the door and leaned out the open window to give Sydney a good-bye kiss on the cheek. "Call me when you're ready."

"Cool. I'll talk to you both tomorrow then," Sydney said as she waved them off and headed inside.

As soon as she closed the front door behind her, Sydney could hear her mother's demanding voice going nonstop. As she kicked her studded Sergio Rossi ballet flats off to the side and dropped her keys in the foyer's community key bowl, Sydney wondered what Keisha Duke was complaining about now.

"I'm tired of asking you, Altimus," Keisha said pointedly.

"Okay, okay, Keish, relax! I just walked in the door. Can a brother please get a minute to breathe before you hit me over the head with your demands?" the twins' stepfather of fifteen years, Altimus Duke, responded wearily.

Tall, dark, and handsome, even when he was tired, Altimus still qualified as a dad most of her classmates wouldn't mind sitting across from at the dinner table every night. Not to mention, on paper Altimus was the modern-day American dream. After hustling his way out of the West End, one of the roughest hoods in Atlanta, he'd continued on to own and operate the most successful chain of luxury car dealerships in the greater Atlanta area. Unfortunately, that was just the story on paper.

Sydney stood quietly outside the kitchen door and listened. "Babe, how long have you been saying you were going to do this? I want you to get on it now or I'm calling a professional to handle it," Keisha threatened in a low voice. A professional? Sydney couldn't imagine what had her mother, who normally saved all her attitude for Sydney and Lauren, so worked up with Altimus. She leaned in closer to the door.

"Is that so," Altimus countered unwaveringly as the ice cubes clinked in what Sydney assumed to be his one-a-day glass of Glenlivet and Drambuie on the rocks.

"Yes, yes, it is. Mark my words, Altimus, you've got two weeks."

"I knew I should have cancelled that damn HGTV channel," Altimus grumbled and pushed back his chair from the kitchen's center island. "Got me living with the black Martha Stewart up in here. . . ."

"Trust, you're going to thank me a month from now when you're relaxing in our fully furnished basement," Mrs. Duke replied confidently. "Now please pass me —"

At the mention of the basement, Sydney broke out in a cold sweat. She immediately headed back to the foyer and grabbed all her shopping bags. Grateful for the plush wall-to-wall carpeting to muffle the sound of her footsteps, Sydney sprinted up the stairs as fast as her legs would carry her and her bags. Hanging a hard left at the top, she headed halfway down the hall and directly into her sister's bedroom without a single breath.

Startled, Lauren dropped the brush she was using to wrap and pin her long auburn/black-streaked weave. "Damn, Syd, do you not know how to knock?" she snapped.

"Yeah, yeah, yeah. I'm sorry," she apologized nervously, dropping her bags and turning to close the door behind her. "Anyway, you are not going to believe this!"

"What?" Lauren asked as she finished tying on her headscarf and turned to look at her sister suspiciously. "Okay, you're scaring me with that face. What is going on? Why are you closing the door?"

"Mom is redoing the basement," Sydney burst out.

"Okay . . . she's been saying that for years. So?" Lauren asked, clearly confused.

"Lauren, she's really serious about it this time. And just think! The pictures of Altimus with Dad from back in the day, the boxes, everything is in the basement!"

A look of confusion passed across Lauren's face. "Wait, I thought you stashed the photo album in your bathroom under the sink," she asked.

"I did. But that's only one album. Can you imagine how much more evidence is down there? How are we going to prove that Altimus had something to do with setting Dice up if . . ."

Lauren's face involuntarily twisted at the sound of her biological father's name. For as long as both girls could remember, Keisha Duke had drilled into their heads that their biological father was worthless, had abandoned his family, and was not to be trusted. Always a daddy's girl, Sydney refused to believe her mother and even sought out a clandestine relationship with Dice on her own. Lauren, on the other hand, bought into the propaganda hook, line, and sinker. Even when Sydney discovered old photos that showed Altimus and Dice used to be best friends (and probably business partners), she still had major trust issues.

"Okay, okay, forget Dice," Sydney implored, noticing her sister's expression. "Think about Jermaine!" Sydney attempted to make the gravity of the situation more personal by reminding her shortsighted sister that her very own boyfriend was also being considered a suspect for the same unsolved crime. "We can't help Jermaine or Dice if all the boxes are destroyed."

Lauren's eyes suddenly became as big as saucers at the sound of their parents walking down the hall. "Oh, my God, Syd, what if Mom notices that her old photo album is missing? You know she'll say something," she whispered. "And then Altimus . . . he'll know."

2
LAUREN

Put it this way: When Lauren cooked up this particular scheme in the middle of her 2:35 A.M. Godiva-chocolate-covered-strawberry eating haze, it really did seem like a good idea. All she had to do was convince the masseuse, the manicurist, and the girl who gave her the custom brown-sugar-lime exfoliating facial to pretend she was in the room getting her spa treatments while she hightailed it on over to the West End to have a look-see for Jermaine. She needed to see him. She needed to make sure he was okay. And most important, she needed him to know that she loved him and had his back, no matter what Dice or Altimus or anybody else was up to, no matter what anyone else thought about it.

This, of course, was something Lauren had been trying

to tell Jermaine ever since he was arrested and named as a suspect in his own brother's murder, and everyone in the hood started making it known that Altimus Duke's fingerprints, not Jermaine's, were probably on the bloody metal rod the killer used to beat Rodney Watson so badly his mama had to have a closed-casket funeral. But Altimus and Keisha weren't making it easy for her to get that message to Jermaine. Though they'd ended the girls' joint punishment and finally stopped holding their cars and cells hostage, Lauren's parents still had the parental supervision programs installed on the Macs that alerted them every time an e-mail was sent to an unauthorized account, and the monthly cell bill was on lockdown, so her texting, e-mail, and phone calls were still limited to computer class, various phone messages made from the front office "emergency" phone, and borrowed cells from friends. Still, despite her desperate pleas for him to reach out, her clandestine calls went unanswered.

She'd expected more of the same when she IM'd Jermaine from a computer in the cheerleading field house just before the football game Friday night, but that didn't stop Lauren from sending him another message. "Why won't you talk to me?" she inquired. As usual, there was no answer, and she needed to get out to the field for the pregame stretch, so she left it alone. She thought for sure that she would faint, though, when Elizabeth Chiclana, a sophomore on the dance squad, called Lauren back over to the computer. "Um, I think this is for you," she sneered, pointing at the computer screen. It was an IM from Jermaine.

"I just need some space to figure things out," the message said simply.

Lauren stared at the screen, mouth agape — temporarily forgetting that Elizabeth was not only watching her every move, but now had evidence of the message right there in front of her to tell the entire world, which was already more enthralled in the Duke family drama than they were the current season of *The Hills*. And Elizabeth was a nosy heiffa, too, so it wouldn't be but two seconds before she reported Jermaine's IM to the entire Brookhaven junior class, or worse, posted it on YoungRichandTriflin.com. *Damn, what the hell was I thinking*, Lauren thought. *Damn, what the hell is he thinking*, Lauren thought some more. *I've got to see him face-to-face*.

Which is how she ended up plotting out her harebrained scheme to get back to the West End — with her mother's help. She was going to talk her way into Keisha's spa appointment, then dip out and get back before Keisha realized she was gone. Keisha, who treated her standing first-Saturday six-hour appointment at Château Elan like it was a CIA stealth mission (details on what she was getting done were apparently top secret and known only at the highest levels), would be none the wiser; she'd be too busy getting pampered to give a damn where her daughter was. Lauren had already worked through all the details, down to paying off the staff on the off chance that Keisha deigned to think about someone other than herself and actually, like, checked up on her daughter. Lauren went to sleep knowing that the hard part was going to be talking her mother into letting her crash her spa date.

Luckily for Lauren, her period was due in only a few days, which meant that her skin was a hot mess. First thing Saturday morning, Lauren swiped a little Vaseline over the offending pimples to make her face look like an oil slick, then hobbled into the kitchen rubbing her lower back, knowing full well that Keisha, dressed impeccably and sipping her coffee, would take immediate note of her skin and back issues. "Oh, you're already up," Lauren said, feigning surprise and tossing in a yawn for good measure.

"My God, you look a wreck," Keisha said, frowning between sips. "Did you fall into a jar of Crisco? And why are you walking like that?"

Lauren sucked her teeth and threw in an eye-roll for good measure to play up her displeasure with her mother's greeting. "Well, good morning to you, too," she snarled.

"I'm just saying —" Keisha started.

"For your information, my back is a little stiff from dancing at the game," Lauren said. She sat across from her mother and moved only slightly to let Edwina place a cold glass of fresh-squeezed orange juice in front of her. "It went into overtime, which meant we were dancing overtime."

"Hmm," Keisha said, eyeing the juice. "Well if you ask me, the last thing you need is that orange juice. "Unless, of course, you actually want more pimples and blackheads on your face. Yuck."

Lauren rolled her eyes again but pushed the orange juice away.

"Well," Keisha said sighing. "You know how sacred my spa appointment is. But it looks like today your back and face need a little bit more TLC than even mine do. Let me call over there and see what miracles they can work for you today."

Lauren said a silent "yes" and danced a jig, if only in her mind. "Aw, Mom, I know how you like to hit the spa solo; I don't want to knock your hustle . . ."

"Oh, let's be clear. You won't be anywhere near me, little girl. Not after I slip into my robe, start sipping my green tea, and fall into the latest issue of *domino*. Trust, I don't want to see your face until I'm about to pull out of the parking lot."

"I love you, too, Keish," Lauren said, showing every last one of her pearly whites.

"Uh-huh. Now go shower and be quick about it. I can't stand rushing, and I don't want to be late," Keisha said, looking at her Philip Stein Teslar timepiece. "Edwina, hand me the phone. I need to have them put some folks on standby for this child."

"Thanks, Mom — you rock," Lauren said, standing up from her chair and hugging Keisha from behind.

Game on.

Marquette? Marquita? Marcia? No matter how many times the facial chick had squeezed Lauren's blackheads and buffed her skin to a high-gloss mahogany, Lauren still couldn't remember her name. Had no reason to, until now. Because the facial chick was intent on giving Lauren a hard time about her escape plans, unlike the masseuse, who happily shoved Lauren's fifty-dollar bill into her lab coat pocket and skipped the hell on for her unexpected but much-appreciated ninety-minute breakfast break.

"But I'm being paid to give you your signature facial," Facial Chick insisted, putting her hands on her hips for emphasis. "That's what I do."

"I know, I know, but come on now, every girl can use a break, right?" Lauren said, putting on her best syrupy smile.

"Uh-huh, right," she said, running her fingers over the folded towels that stood sentry on the table next to the facial table. "I'm going to go ahead and let you disrobe and get comfortable, then I'll be right back in to service you."

"Wait," Lauren said, putting her hand on Facial Chick's shoulder. Immediately, she regretted it. Could have been the fact that homegirl looked at her hand like she was going to rip it off Lauren's limbs, could have been that Lauren had long ago assessed that she could not take Facial Chick on her best day, even hopped up on multivitamins and Red Bull. But whatever it was, Lauren knew she better get to some fast talking before this girl a) kicked her ass, b) blocked her chance to go find Jermaine, and c) told Keisha what she was up to. "Sorry, sorry — I don't mean to be inappropriate," Lauren said. "I shouldn't have touched you. It's just that I really need to skip outta here. I mean, you're young, you know what it's like to be on lockdown and have your parents constantly blocking, right?"

"Go on," Facial Chick said.

"Well, I really need to go see my boyfriend, but, well, put it this way: My parents think I need to find another man."

"And I take it you don't agree, huh?"

"Right."

"Well, personally, I happen to think your parents have a damn good point," Facial Chick said, folding her arms.

Lauren didn't quite know what to say, which explained why her mouth was hanging open. Facial Chick was amused.

"Well, my fifty dollars says you try to see things my way," Lauren said, recovering.

"Girl, please. Fifty dollars? Your mother will give me double that in tips after I finish fixing your face."

"Okay, well then, take her hundred and my hundred, too, for doing nothing but keeping quiet about me leaving while my mother's getting worked on. If you've ever been in love, you'll understand why I need to do this, and outside the prying eyes of my parents." And with that, Lauren reached into her robe, pulled out a crisp hundred-dollar bill, and let it hang in the pocket of space between the two of them. Facial Chick looked down at the hundred, and, after brief consideration, slowly pulled the money from between Lauren's fingertips.

"You got about five hours before your moms is finished," Facial Chick said, snapping the hundred-dollar bill and holding it up to the light before tossing an evil eye at Lauren and stepping out of the room.

Lauren rolled her eyes at the door, smoothed her hair, and tipped on out of the swank room. She said a silent prayer that she'd have an easier time at her destination than she was having at the beginning of her journey.

It was a little after eleven when the train pulled into the West End Station, and already the sun was pounding down on the busy sidewalk, like it was late summer instead of November. Still, Lauren pulled her jacket just a little tighter around her chest. Despite having been to the West End enough times to find her way comfortably from the station to Jermaine's house, the neighborhood still made her feel like it would swallow her whole before she made it to the corner. But she pushed forward anyway, eyes darting — partly in search of Jermaine, partly in search of trouble.

She found it — not him — at Pride, the fried-fish joint where she and Jermaine had gone the day Altimus caught Lauren hanging with her man. Except this time, it wasn't Altimus's sinister hand that caught her off-guard: It was Brandi's. Lauren jumped when the girl, Jermaine's ex, tapped her on the shoulder. "Well, didn't expect to see you here, slumming in the daylight. Usually, the Dukes do all their dirty in the dark," Brandi sniffed.

Lauren felt her heart go into overdrive; she could practically taste the adrenaline in her throat. "Uh, Brandi, right?" Lauren stammered.

Brandi said nothing.

Lauren swallowed hard but made a quick decision to play it cool a) to keep Brandi from beating her ass and b) in hopes that the girl would have mercy on her and provide a clue as to where she might be able to find Jermaine, and quick. "How you been?" Lauren said, this time, a little more confidently. "Haven't seen you in a while."

"Why would you see me?" Brandi snapped. "You ain't from 'round here. As a matter of fact, you ain't got no business 'round here now. What you want? Didn't your daddy make clear his little princess isn't supposed to be around these parts?"

"I came to see about Jermaine," Lauren said as she willed her hands to stop shaking. They didn't.

"Came to see about Jermaine, huh? Well, from what I understand, he's doing just fine, so there's no need for you to worry your pretty little weaved head," Brandi said, laughing. "He's being well cared for."

Well cared for, Lauren said to herself. *Just what the hell was that supposed to mean?* "Oh, really? And who's caring for him?" Lauren said, finding her voice and raising it a decibel or two to match Brandi's, a move that turned a few heads in the half-crowded restaurant.

"Like I said, that's really none of your concern now, is it?"

"You know what? It *is* my concern because Jermaine is my friend and I want to make sure my friend is okay."

"It's because of you that your 'friend' is lying low," Brandi said, emphasizing the word "friend" with hand quotes. She leaned in so close Lauren could smell the Breathsaver on her tongue. "Some kinda friend if your actions do more harm than good."

"I don't know what you're talking about," Lauren said, squaring her shoulders and pushing her nose slightly into the air.

"Oh, yeah? You don't know what I'm talking about, huh?" Brandi said, this time loud enough to draw the attention of the entire room.

"Ain't that nothing? That boy's body ain't even warm in his grave yet, and the person responsible for putting him there don't even remember it happening," Brandi said to her audience, a clear attempt to get them hyped.

"I . . . I didn't say I didn't remember Rodney," Lauren stumbled. "I'm just saying I didn't really have anything to do —"

"Right, I know, I know — you ain't had nothing to do with it, right? Must be nice being able to go on back to Buckhead and pretend. Jermaine told me you were trying to be an actress; but funny, he didn't mention you were so good," Brandi snapped, folding her arms. The murmurs of Brandi's audience started to get a little louder, the crowd started getting a little closer, and Lauren started to get a lot more nervous.

"Look, Brandi, I didn't come here to start anything with you —" Lauren said.

"Just being here in my neighborhood means you looking to start something," Brandi snapped, her proclamation punctuated by "I know that's right" and "You betta tell it" from the audience, which was getting steadily closer. Brandi stepped up to Lauren and raised her hand with such quickness, Lauren thought she was going to hit her. But at the last second, Brandi psyched her out and scratched her head instead. Brandi smirked; Lauren gulped.

The hand on Lauren's shoulder made her practically jump out of her Sevens. "Lauren," the man said, grabbing her. "Come on, let's take a walk outside."

A look of sheer terror crossed Lauren's face. She'd already sized up Brandi and accepted that it was a no-win situation for her; at most, Lauren prayed she could get in a few good licks before Brandi stomped her into a stupor. But a grown man? Wasn't no way.

Lauren tried to tug her arm from the stranger's grasp, but his grip was firm. "Just walk. Trust me on this," he said, pulling her toward the door, despite Lauren's pathetic attempt at a struggle. As the man pushed her out the door, she heard Brandi announce to her audience, "Saved again. Next time, fam might not be around to save you, sweetie. I'll see you soon. Real soon."

Lauren's eyes darted back and forth across the sidewalk; she silently willed a cop to come riding through the street and see this crazy man holding on to her arm and, like, save her or something. Then she tried yelling. "Get your hands off me!" she screamed, finally snatching her arm away.

"Look, Lauren, calm the hell down — no one's going to hurt you. I'm just trying to help you here, before someone does hurt you," the man said.

"How do you know my name?" Lauren asked, clearly

taken aback. She'd never seen him before, but still, he looked familiar somehow.

"You were named after me."

What the . . .

"Humph, you didn't know, did you? That you have an uncle you were named after? Makes sense. Keisha always went out of her way to cut off folks if they weren't down with her program."

"What are you talking about?" Lauren demanded. "And how do you know my mother?"

"I'm your uncle Larry," he said, extending his hand. "Actually, Laurence is my real name, which is why your name is Lauren."

Lauren looked at his hand like it was a hot coal, refusing to shake it. Uncle Laurence wasn't fazed. "Walk with me to my car."

"I'm not getting into a car with you. I don't know you from Adam," Lauren seethed. "But since you know my mother, maybe you know my father? Altimus? 'Cause from what I'm told, you may not want to mess with his family."

Uncle Larry smirked. "Yeah, smart girl. You Keisha's daughter, all right," he said. "Look here, Lauren, listen to your Uncle Larry and get on back to Buckhead. You don't want no part of the hood."

"You're right. I just came here to check up on my friend," she said, looking over her shoulder to see where Brandi and her audience were. No surprise, Brandi had her face pressed against the glass, mean-mugging. "Like I said, I didn't come looking for trouble."

"No matter. Somehow, trouble always manages to find them Dukes," Uncle Larry said. "But not today, not you. Now like I said, get on back to Buckhead and let Altimus and Keisha and Dice deal with all this mess, okay? Your friend is gonna be just fine — all the better if you just lay low."

"Wait, you know Jermaine?" Lauren asked, letting down her guard, if only a bit.

Uncle Larry looked over his own shoulder this time. "Yeah, I know your boyfriend. And I also know it's not safe for either one of you in this neighborhood right now. So believe me, sweetie, it's time to go on home."

"Well, have you seen him? I really need to . . ."

"I'll let him know," Uncle Larry said, smiling. "Now if you ain't gonna let me drive you home, then you're back on that train. It'll be here directly," he said, practically shoving her toward the steps leading down to the station.

"But one last thing. How can I get in touch with you?" Lauren said, pushing back against his hand.

"Call your father — your real one. He knows how to find me," Uncle Larry answered, staring at the door of Pride, his eyes meeting Brandi's. "Now go on."

And with that, Lauren tugged her jacket around her body, pulled her purse under her arm, and hightailed it down the stairs toward the track where her train was arriving. She hopped from one foot to the other and looked at her TAG — it was 11:30. The train doors could hardly open fast enough before Lauren practically ran through them, searching for a seat as close to the conductor as she could get without sitting on his lap.

If she weren't so preoccupied finding that seat, Lauren might've noticed the long shadow Jermaine's hoody cast on the wall just beyond the station's Coca-Cola vending machine.

3
SYDNEY

"Hey, wait up!" a voice called out from across the empty parking lot as Sydney tossed her bag over her shoulder and locked the door on her recently washed silver Saab. At six-thirty in the morning, it was still too early for most Brookhaven students to be awake let alone rolling up to school. Sydney looked cautiously over her shoulder in the direction of the sound of approaching footsteps and disengaged the safety lock on the tiny can of pepper spray attached to her key chain.

"Oh, hey," Sydney replied with a relieved smile as Jason Danden's familiar figure came into view from behind a couple of parked cars several rows over. An impressive six foot something, Jason's smooth cocoa-colored skin, perfect smile, and chiseled physique, noticeable even under his heather-gray flannel shirt, immediately set the butterflies in her stomach aflutter. Sydney instinctively ran a hand over her head to smooth any flyaway curls. After weeks of dodging, Sydney was surprised at how happy she was to talk to him again.

"Morning, sunshine, don't you look pretty today," Jason offered with a smile as he finally stood directly in front of her with his book bag on one shoulder and football helmet in the other hand. "The color is hot on you."

"Aww, thanks, Jason," she replied, shyly pulling the neck on her purple TSE cashmere sweater dress close against the early morning chill.

"Just telling it like I see it," he said simply. "So, long time no speak . . . Everything been good?" he asked before looking away slightly.

Sydney looked down at the ground and shuffled her feet. "Yeah, right? Guess I've been kinda busy. . . ."

"True. These morning and afternoon practices have got me running, too," he said with a slight shrug. "But, er, um, if you saw our last game, you know why we got to be out here as much as possible," he joked.

"Whatever," Sydney giggled at his self-deprecating sense of humor. "If it makes it any better, you aren't the only one trying to stage a comeback. I have some major catching up to do in Global if I don't want Dr. Pitts to call me out again in class this week. Which is why I'm up here so early. Figured I'd hit the library while it's still quiet."

"And you're sure you couldn't do that damage control from the comfort of your bed?" he continued with a grin.

"Oh, I'm sure," she replied emphatically as the two started to walk in tandem toward the school entrance. What Sydney didn't bother to say was that, in addition to the ongoing Marcus drama, ever since she'd learned of Keisha's plans to clean out the basement, she'd been totally unable to sleep or relax, let alone study in the house. Convinced that Altimus was going to come storming into her room at any moment and threaten her within an inch of her life, Sydney spent the entire weekend trying to figure out how to get the photo album back downstairs and into the box without either parent noticing. Unfortunately, now that Mrs. Duke was officially HGTV obsessed, she ran in and out of the basement taking measurements and trying to figure out all the details of her upcoming renovation day and night.

"Well, I just hope that you haven't been stressed out about what happened at the Gala or anything," Jason hedged as he slowed down at the base of the staircase from the lot to the school's main entrance. Jason reached out and gently touched Sydney's arm.

Secretly relieved that he'd actually brought up the awkward topic, Sydney tried to keep her response light. "Well, it sure hasn't helped," she laughed ruefully.

"Yeah, it sure didn't look that good from a distance," he stated simply.

"Oh, trust me, looks are nothing compared to hearing it being discussed by people who don't even know me," Sydney continued, not wanting to imagine what he'd heard about her around the school halls.

"One thing about New Yorkers," Jason started slowly, "we're always loyal to our home team. And we're known to believe nothing we hear and only half of what we see."

"Is that so? Well, now that I'm a free agent, maybe I'll start looking into switching teams," Sydney suggested with a coy grin.

"All I'm saying is, you'd be surprised how different life can be on a winning squad," he flirted back and continued to softly stroke her arm.

As the two locked eyes, Sydney's entire body started to tingle. With all the drama leading up to her actual breakup, it had been a long time since she'd gotten the "uh-oh" feeling from Marcus. Thoughts of what Jason's hands might feel like running up and down the rest of her body sent Sydney's hormones into overdrive. "I'm so sure," she offered, boldly stepping closer to Jason. In response, he lowered his eyes and smiled invitingly.

As the tension was reaching the boiling point, the sound of two cars blaring the Hot 107.9 A-Team morning show suddenly raced into the lot. Jason looked past Sydney and shook his head. "I swear Ryan and Keyshawn are going to kill themselves one of these days," he said before turning back. "Well, I guess I better go. The co-captains are actually supposed to be on the field *before* the rest of the squad," Jason offered as he looked down at his leather-banded Swiss Army watch.

"Well, I won't keep you, then. Thanks for walking me over," Sydney responded.

"My pleasure," he asserted with a smile. "Good luck with Global."

" 'Preciate it. Good luck with practice." Sydney returned the smile and started up the long steps.

"Hey, Syd," Jason called out suddenly. Sydney turned around and looked at him expectantly. "You still got my number, right?" he asked.

Fighting against the huge grin that threatened to erupt on her face, Sydney nodded before answering, "Sure do."

"Well, now that you're a free agent, you should definitely use it."

"Thank you, Jesus," Sydney exhaled as she tapped in the final period on the last sentence of her Modern English Lit paper on Zora Neale Hurston. She leaned back in the comfy ergonomic computer lab chair and closed her eyes in relief.

"Somebody looks like they could use a good massage," a familiar voice teased softly behind her left ear.

Sydney's eyelids flew open as she sat up straight in the chair. "Excuse you?" she asked defensively with much attitude.

"Whoa, whoa, slow down, Syd. I didn't mean anything," Marcus said, stepping back and throwing up both hands.

"What do you want, Marcus?" Sydney hissed as she hurriedly began to save her document to the file and shut down the computer.

"I just want to talk," he said in a lowered voice, bending down beside her to avoid their conversation being overheard by the twenty pairs of ears that perked up as he walked over to Sydney. The smell of his cologne immediately filled Sydney's nostrils.

"I thought I made it clear that I don't have anything to talk to you about," Sydney replied through clenched teeth. She was also acutely aware of the eerie silence that filled the room in lieu of the normal clacking on the keyboards.

"You did," he concurred. "But there's something that I want to say if you'll just give me five seconds," he implored, softly pressing his hand over hers as she attempted to pick up her bag.

Refusing to look him in the eyes, Sydney instead focused on his hand. "Don't you think you said everything there was to say at the Gala? Or is there another smart Jason comment that you'd like to share?" she whispered, although she didn't make any move to shake his hand off of hers.

"I'm sorry, Syd," Marcus blurted out. "I'm sorry about the Gala, I'm sorry about yesterday, I'm sorry about everything that has happened since school started. It was totally my ego that created this mess, and you've done nothing to deserve it."

"You got that right," Sydney muttered, still looking away.

"I want . . . I mean, even my mom misses you. She keeps asking me where you are and why she hasn't heard you call the house lately. I don't know what to say or how to explain —"

"Why don't you just tell her that you prefer the company of hoochies and sluts to the girl that's had your back for the past four years," Sydney snapped, cutting him off in midsentence.

"You know that's not true, Sydney," he asserted in a slightly raised voice. Sydney looked at him with raised eyebrows. He quickly cleared his throat and started again. "At the end of the day, there's no one that I want to be with more than you."

"Hmm, no offense, Marcus, but I've heard this all before," Sydney replied, finally pulling her hand away and standing up to leave. "I gotta go." Sydney turned and marched toward the door.

Refusing to give up, Marcus followed right behind her. "Come on, Sydney, give me a break here," he begged as soon as the door to the lab closed behind them. He desperately grabbed her arm to make her stop. "I *am* sorry. I can't stop thinking about how I could have done things differently . . . how I *will* do things differently. Please just listen to what I'm saying. I mean it."

Sydney turned around slowly. Her ears were hearing all the right things, but it just wasn't enough. She thought about how hard she'd worked over the years to be the "perfect girlfriend" and show her appreciation for "such a good black man." She vividly recalled how insecure and paranoid she'd become those last couple of weeks before the scandalous affair was discovered. And most damaging, how he tried to play her in front of everybody with his remarks about Jason when he was the one with the secret agenda. "I think I need some time, Marcus," she said at last, realizing that for once she had the upper hand in the situation, that this time around, Sydney was the one with options. "You really hurt me. And seeing you leave school with Caroline and Trina last week? I mean really."

"Caroline and Trina are trying to set up a mentorship program at the Girls Club in Alpharetta. They wanted me to introduce them to the director of programming at the Boys Club where I volunteer. That's all that was, Syd," Marcus immediately explained.

"I see. Well, that's good to know," Sydney said, looking down the empty hallway uncomfortably.

"But anyway, I hear what you're saying. If you need time that's fine. I won't pressure you," Marcus finally conceded with a look of defeat.

"I appreciate it," Sydney said simply as she checked her diamond-studded Deco Park II Michele watch. "Listen, um,

I gotta go. I want to catch up with Carmen before my Art History class starts."

"Yeah, sure. . . . Well, thanks for listening. I know I was about five minutes too long," he joked, trying to lighten up their good-bye.

And about five minutes too late, Sydney thought smugly as she walked away with barely a wave.

The first thing Sydney noticed when she pulled her car into the family's four-car garage was the missing burgundy Benz CL5. Saying a silent Hail Mary, she threw the gear into park, grabbed her bag, and hurried inside. "Hel-lo? Anybody home," Sydney called out hesitantly as she entered the kitchen from the garage.

"Just me, Miss Sydney," the Duke's live-in housekeeper, Edwina, replied from in front of the oven where, from the escaping aroma, she was baking the family favorite, spinach frittata.

"Hey, Edwina" Sydney replied as she took her off purple-and-gray patent leather Via Spiga mary janes and dropped them in the shoe basket at the door. Noticing the basement door closed for the first time in days, Sydney prayed again that her initial suspicion was correct — Mrs. Duke was not home. "Um, is my mom here?"

"No, miss. She chipped a nail while working in the basement earlier. So, I believe she went to the salon to have it fixed," Edwina answered as she headed over to the Sub-Zero fridge and pulled out Sydney's favorite after-school snack. "She should be back shortly."

Desperate to seize the opportunity to get the photo album down to the basement, Sydney dashed out of the room before Edwina could even offer her the plate of freshly cut pineapple and watermelon slices. Taking the steps two at a time, Sydney's heart raced as she finally burst into her immaculate bedroom at the end of the hall. Barely pausing to catch her breath, she tossed her bag on the bed and headed into the bathroom. There tucked behind bottles of Pink Conditioning shampoo, a bag of cotton balls, her favorite Clarins body products, and boxes of Tampax, she found the huge old leather-bound photo album she'd snagged from one of Keisha's boxes of personal items a few weeks ago.

"Aha," she mumbled, pulling it out and starting back toward her bedroom. Halfway through the bathroom door, she stopped and looked down at the album. With a split-second decision, she flipped to the middle, removed the single most incriminating photo in the album — Keisha and Dice's official wedding photo, where Altimus was the best man — and shoved it back in the cabinet. Just in case.

Unsure how long she had until her mother returned, without further delay Sydney raced back down the stairs. She paused momentarily outside the kitchen door to listen for voices in case she had missed the garage door opening while she was upstairs in her bathroom. Confident that the coast was clear, Sydney finally walked into the kitchen.

"You okay? You don't want no food, Miss Sydney?" Edwina asked from the small table where she sat cutting up vegetables for the dinner salad. She stopped to point at the plate on the counter.

"In a minute," Sydney replied as she beelined for the basement door. " I just need to grab something from downstairs right quick."

"Okay. If you need help, let me know. . . ."

"Mmm-hmm," she murmured in response as she opened the door and flipped on the light. "I'll be fine."

Sydney started down the stairs slowly. When she finally reached the bottom, she looked around in complete shock. The normally cluttered room officially looked like a bomb had hit. Everything was thrown all over the place. Clearly, Altimus intended to go through every single item before he allowed Keisha to dump it. "What a mess," Sydney muttered as she scanned the floor for the pile of boxes in which she'd originally found the photo album. After a minute or two, she noticed the pair of boxes pushed under Altimus's old bench-press machine. Trying not to trip, she carefully picked her way over to the other side of the room.

As she made her way over the last pile of junk between her and the boxes, Sydney heard the sound of the garage door opening. Panicking, she tossed the album into the fray and made a dash for the door. But common sense told her that when Keisha or Altimus found the album haphazardly thrown on top a pile of old clothes it would be just as bad if not worse than it just being missing. At least that way, there was a chance they might assume it was lost during the original move years prior. Sydney did a 180-degree turn, retrieved the album, and bolted up the stairs.

Just as she stepped out and closed the door behind her, Mrs. Duke appeared in the garage entrance wearing a hot pink Juicy track suit and holding three large Crate & Barrel shopping bags. As she placed them on the ground, the sound of clinking glasses escaped. "Hey, Mom," Sydney exclaimed a little too brightly.

Keisha looked up as she bent over to take off her leather Hogan sneakers. "Hay is for horses, Sydney," she answered automatically, flipping her honey blonde weave over her left shoulder. "And why are you yelling? There's nothing wrong with my hearing."

"Sorry," Sydney returned in a more normal tone.

"That's better," she said, grabbing her bags and heading over to the counter directly in front of Sydney. "I swear I hate going to the nail shop late in the afternoon. It's always so crowded," she huffed as she put the bags on the counter. Edwina automatically stood up, grabbed the bags, and disappeared into the pantry to put the items away.

"Sorry to hear about it," Sydney said, trying to steady the

nervous tremor in her voice. More than anything, she wished Keisha would pass so she could move away from the basement door.

Finally, noticing the stressed look on Sydney's face and the large book behind her back, Mrs. Duke's eyes narrowed. "What are you doing?" she asked suspiciously.

"Oh, um, nothing. I was just grabbing my after-school snack and heading back up to my room to study," she stuttered. She stepped forward and anxiously grabbed the large plate of fruit still sitting on the counter and placed it on top of the photo album as quickly as possible.

"Is that so," Keisha said as she looked from the album to the basement door where Sydney was standing and back again.

"Yes, ma'am," Sydney answered, realizing that if she didn't make a speedy exit Keisha's twenty-twenty would spot the album's distinct markings. "Got a big test on Friday, can't afford to waste any time. Especially with all the party planning I still have to do." Sydney took big steps toward the door. "I'll see you at dinner, okay?" she said as she darted into the living room.

"Oh, okay," Mrs. Duke responded to Sydney's retreating back as she slowly walked over to the closed basement door. As soon as Sydney was completely out of sight, Keisha opened the door and found the light on.

4
LAUREN

My God, Donald's got to get a hold of himself, Lauren practically said out loud. There he was, up there on the Grace Temple AME Church of Christ choir-rehearsal stage, fa la la la la-ing and smiling at the other singers and swinging his head like he was in the school glee club. Yeah, um, the "I'm not gay, really" charade? To the wind. Donald came back from his "punishment" at the all-boys' school in Chicago early (his father — finally catching on to the grapevine gossip that Trinity Men's Academy was practically the citadel of gay pride — pulled his boy out and reenrolled him at Brookhaven Prep) and now Donald was a changed man: He was more gay than ever and clearly willing to go public with it, despite the fact that his father threatened to force him into West Point and then the Marines to, well, you know, *really* make a man out of him or something. The thought of unlimited buff boy toys made Donald hot, but he had no interest in taking up arms or, worse, waking up before sunrise to, as he put it, "Pull on those perfectly dreadful overstarched uniforms." Lucky for him, Donald's mother couldn't wrap her mind around an image of her son running through some foreign country with an assault weapon in his hand, either, so she deaded the whole "off to the Marines with you" mantra her husband had adopted, threatening to divorce Mr. Aller, take half his money, and tell a reporter friend of hers at the *Atlanta Journal-Constitution* a few details about the celebrated attorney's Internet porn addiction. Now, Donald, empowered by his mother's hardball stance, was on a damn rampage. Which explained why he was practically twirling off the rehearsal stage.

"He so wants me," Donald said as he walked up to Lauren, winking at the choir director and tossing in a "tootles" wave for good measure. "Can't touch this," he hissed, making a sizzling sound for effect as he rubbed his booty. Lauren sucked her teeth and shook her head at his outrageous shenanigans. "Anyway, smooches," Donald said to Lauren, air kissing each side of her face. "It's good to finally see you again. Where you been hiding?"

"Oh, well, you know, just maintaining," Lauren said half-heartedly as she straightened Donald's tie and brushed imaginary lint off his choir-issued red velvet jacket.

Actually, "maintaining" was a really enthusiastic assessment of the situation, considering Lauren had hardly eaten or slept since her run-in with Brandi and Uncle Larry in the West End. She had replayed the scene over and over in her mind, and had seriously considered borrowing someone's phone to call Aunt Lorraine, but it was too risky and she did not want to have to explain to anyone — or, worse, read all about it on YoungRichandTriflin.com. As it was, she was already doing damage control over the message from Jermaine that somehow got forwarded "mysteriously," according to Elizabeth Chiclana, to the Web site. The resulting fallout was downright ugly:

> Looks like one of Brookhaven's own just can't get enough of the hard-knock life; despite numerous warnings from her Daddy Warbucks to stay away from the dirty dirty, she's been making a go of reconnecting with her West End boo. Too bad the feeling's not mutual; sources tell YRT that booby boo is looking for a "little space" while he tries to get that dirt (and potential murder charge) off his shoulder, and there just isn't enough room for him to put his "dukes" up.

Lauren was so embarrassed by the posting that she convinced Keisha she was too sick to go to school on Monday and Tuesday. When Keisha called Dr. Robertson to make an appointment Wednesday morning, Lauren "miraculously" started feeling good enough to make it to class, but she stalked the halls with a snarl so fierce nobody dared speak beyond a standard "What up?" much less ask details on what was going on with Jermaine.

Try as she might, Lauren couldn't shake Sydney, though. In her sister's eyes, Lauren had violated their pinkie-swear agreement. On the night of their parents' anniversary celebration, the two of them made a pact not to speak to anyone but each other about Rodney's murder, or the potential involvement of Altimus, Dice, and Jermaine, or especially what they had found out about their parents' marriage. Even those conversations, they agreed, should take place outside of Keisha's prying ears at the house, either at school or on their way back home in the car. Nowhere else. And especially out of earshot of everyone else.

Which explained why Sydney was all in Lauren's face before she could even pull her Saab down the circular driveway as the two made their way to choir rehearsal, demanding to know what Lauren had done to set Keisha off.

"What do you mean, 'What did I do?'" Lauren charged back.

"You were trying to reach out to Jermaine again," Sydney said through her teeth. "I thought we agreed you would stay away from him until things calmed down."

"For your information, I haven't seen him," Lauren snipped.

"But you talked to him — I saw it on YRT," Sydney said. "You should have known it would be just a matter of time before it got back to Mom. She was stalking around the house just now like she's a detective on *Law & Order*. Shoot, she almost busted me out with the photo album."

"What? She knows you have it?" Lauren asked, fear making her head hot. She reached over, turned on the air conditioner, and unfastened the belt on her Heatherette flight jacket.

"I was trying to put it back in the basement, and she came home before I could get it back down there. I swear my heart was in my throat when she started walking over trying to see what I had in my hand. I got out of there in time, I think, but still. We don't need to make her any more suspicious than she already is. Try to stay off YRT, okay?"

"I'm not doing anything to get on YRT," Lauren insisted. She decided that instant to keep her trip to the West End, and her introduction to Uncle Larry, to herself.

"Whatever, Lauren," Sydney said. "Just lay off calling Jermaine until we can figure some stuff out. And try to keep this on the hush; nobody, especially your little friends, needs to know about what's going on."

Now Lauren was trying to decide whether that directive should include Donald, her ace confident.

"Maintaining, huh?" Donald asked, clearly not convinced. "I heard a little chatter about what's been going on with you while I was, um, 'away,'" he continued, making imaginary quote marks with his fingers. "So tell me about this boy you got caught with on the other side of town."

See? There just wasn't any good reason why Donald should know all Lauren's business, seeing as he'd been incommunicado in an entirely different region of the country for the past month. Except that big-mouthed Keisha had been all up in Sheer, telling Toni, her hair stylist, to keep an eye on her twins because "It takes a village to keep these little girls in check and out of the hood."

"Kids these days — this MTV culture is going to be the death of this generation," Toni clucked, sipping his tea and tossing Keisha a knowing look. But not because he actually believed what she was saying to be true; in the mind of Toni, who styled the hair of Buckhead's black high society, Keisha's girls were just apples off the old Keisha tree — new-money problematic. His clients were watching her. And warning their kids to watch the girls, too. Keisha, for all her street smarts, was too new to catch on. Lauren got it, though, and so did her sister.

"God, I don't know why Keisha can't talk about something else with her friends besides my damn business," Lauren huffed.

"Oooh, potty mouth in the House of the Lord," Donald squealed, holding his hand up to his mouth. "The shame of it all."

"What's a shame is that you weren't even in the state and you know what was going on with my tragic soap opera saga," Lauren sighed.

"Come on, honey, you know your boyfriend had to keep up with the happenings. But these sorry heiffas around here are good for getting it all twisted, so I'm coming to you to get the real deal," Donald said. "Besides, you know I'm happy to run interference between you and all these nosy haters. Just tell Donald baby what's really hood."

Lauren took Donald by the hand and led him to a set of folding chairs far away from the rest of the choir, which was preening and prepping for their morning service entrance. She smoothed down her charcoal gray silk Elie Tahari dress and sat on the cold metal seat. "Honestly, D, I don't know sometimes if I'm coming or going," Lauren whispered, looking down at her hot-pink box-toe pumps. "I haven't heard from Jermaine in weeks, and as far as I know, he's either still being blamed for his brother's death, or looking for his killer, or both, which means he could be in a lot of trouble and Altimus may be involved in all of it."

"Whoa, whoa — slow down. Murder and mayhem? When did all of that enter the equation? And what does Altimus have to do with it?" Donald gasped.

Lauren looked at Donald and rolled her eyes. "Okay, why don't you tell me what you think you know, so I can fill in the real details," she said, exasperated. Who knew what rumors were floating through the Buckhead Jack & Jill set.

Donald took a deep breath and let it whirl. "What I had heard was that you were wrapped around a catfish sandwich at a bar in the SWATS, and Altimus dragged you outta the hood drunk and half high after an afternoon of cavorting with some boy with a record a half mile long. I also heard that you will never see the light of day again if you ever get caught over in the West End and that Sydney finally caught on to the fact that Marcus is more of a dog than ten of Mike Vick's pit bulls. . . ."

Lauren huffed and cut Donald short.

"What? Were at least some of the details right?" he asked.

"Well at least Keisha's managed to keep some of the details to herself — the stuff that she's got a part in. I guess I should be happy about that much, huh?" Lauren huffed.

"Well, dang, you mean there's more?" Donald said, genuinely surprised.

"I mean, there's way more to the story than what you heard and what people think they know," Lauren said quietly.

"Well, do tell."

"I don't know if I'm ready yet," Lauren said.

"Lauren, what in the hell are you talking about?" Donald gasped. "It's me, Donald. We don't have *any* secrets, remember? I know everything about you, and you know pretty much everything about me. Have I ever let you down? Told anyone about Dice? Or dished about Keisha and all her mess? When you were trying to be the queen of BET, did I tell anybody about your tryouts? Does anybody up in this piece, besides your twin sister, know you're still a virgin? I mean, come on. I know how to keep a secret."

"Well, at the rate we're going, I might die a virgin. I can't find Jermaine, and if I do end up finding him, Altimus might kill him dead, which could quite possibly mean he's solely responsible for making Jermaine's mother a childless mom."

"Hold up. What do you mean Altimus would be responsible? Are you saying Altimus laid out Jermaine's brother? All this time, I thought we were talking about Dice."

"I didn't say that," Lauren said, her eyes darting across the room to get a visual on who might be listening to their conversation. To her relief, everyone seemed pretty consumed with preparing for their morning service entrance. "And for God's sake, keep your voice down."

"Well then, stop playing and tell me what you're trying to say," Donald said, leaning in conspiratorially.

Lauren made another eye sweep of the room, then leaned into Donald. She started from the beginning, explaining how she met Jermaine after her failed video dancer tryout, and how they started dating on the DL because she was afraid of what people might think of where he lived and how much money he didn't have, and how she fell in love with him because he didn't put on any airs and he liked her for her and was brave enough to be with her despite who her father was.

"Which is why I need to find him. I'm afraid that he's going to get pinned for something my father may have done," Lauren said.

"Wait, I'm confused," Donald said. "Which father?"

"Altimus! Damn, Donald!" Lauren said, annoyed. "When do I ever call Dice my dad?"

"Look, I'm just trying to get the facts right, okay — don't get loud with me." Donald huffed. "All that I've ever known about your stepfather is that he's a solid businessman who spent years on the come-up, and now he's running things. Anything outside of that, well, it's news to me. But if you're saying he's a gangsta for real? Oh, my . . ."

" 'Oh, my,' would be the understatement of life," Lauren said. "Personally, I don't know if Altimus is involved, or if Dice had something to do with this. My money's on Dice —" Lauren started. She stopped talking when she got a visual of Sydney, who was tossing her a look from across the room while trying desperately to look like she actually gave a crap about whatever Alicia Smart and Nory Cole, two choir members who served on the Jack & Jill holiday charity committee under Sydney, were talking about. She was tugging at her ear and looking over her shoulder in Lauren's direction, giving her the "what the hell are you talking about" eye. Honestly, Lauren was always amazed that Sydney instinctively knew when she was messing up, and Lauren was messing up for sure.

"Look, can we talk about this some other time?" Lauren said, trying, albeit unsuccessfully, to turn her attention away from Sydney's angry eyes.

"We're most definitely going to talk about Altimus and Dice and all this mess later, but right now, I want to talk about this Jermaine and why you're not out there trying to get your man."

"Don't you think I've tried?" Lauren asked, finally standing up and turning her back to Sydney. "I call his house, and his mother acts like I'm the damn law calling to cart her child off to prison. I would assume that he hasn't returned any of my phone calls because his moms isn't giving him the message, but he hasn't answered any of my e-mails, hasn't acknowledged any of my writing on his Facebook wall, and outside of that message that showed up on YRT, he hasn't texted me, either. It's like he's dropped off the face of the earth."

"Look, if you really like this boy like you say you do, walking around here moping with your bottom lip dragging on the ground isn't going to get him back. You need to be proactive. Take a page from me."

"A page from you, huh?" Lauren said, smiling. "And from what book would that be in? Who are you, Dr. Phil now? Just because you went out on a coupla dates?" Lauren laughed.

"Oh, girl, you know I been had the gift of figuring out these little boys. Let's just say that while I was away, I picked up a few more pointers on how to catch a man and reel him in," Donald laughed, mockingly catching a fish with an imaginary pole.

"Whatever, Donald!" Lauren laughed.

"Whatever, hell." Donald said. "I'll tell you what you need to do: You need to stop worrying about what everybody else has to say about it and go on ahead and get your man. If you don't care about what kinda money he got in his pocket, or where his mama is from, or what his daddy is doing, why should you care about what other people think?"

"It's much more complicated than that, and you know it because I just told you . . ." Lauren began. But Sydney's touch made her body go cold.

"Sydney, darling — long time no see," Donald said, giving Sydney a weak wave. He was still pissed at her for dragging him out of the closet, but he was getting over it. Kinda.

"Uh, hey, Donald, how you been?" Sydney stammered. "It's, um, good to see you. Lauren, can I talk to you for a minute?" she said, pulling her sister's arm.

"Can't this wait a minute? I'm just trying to catch up with my old friend," Lauren said, forcing a smile to her face.

"I'm sorry. I know this is the first time you're seeing Donald since his, um, return, but it's really important," Sydney insisted, her grip tightening around Lauren's elbow.

"Whoa, cowgirl, just give me a couple more minutes to visit with my girl, and then she's all —" Donald stopped his words cold and then started grinning like a giggly schoolgirl. He waved his hand wildly and motioned someone to come over. Before Lauren and Sydney could get a good read of who Donald's friend was, he'd already bounded across the rehearsal room and fallen into Donald's arms.

"I'm so glad you made it — it's great to see you!" the boy practically shouted. By now, the music in the room stopped playing, the choir members and their various clingers-on had stopped talking — hell, the birds outside stopped chirping.

"It's good to see you, too, baby," Donald exclaimed. He leaned in and gave the boy a lingering kiss on the cheek, then grabbed his hand and swung it back and forth a few times. The collective gasp changed the air pressure in the room. Sydney and Lauren, eyes furrowed, looked at each other and then back at Donald, like he was a brother from another planet.

"Lauren? I want you to meet Dennis. Dennis Brooks. I met him at Trinity — he's my ex-roommate's brother. Goes to Morehouse. Isn't he cute?"

"Uh, nice to meet you, er, Dennis," Lauren said, shaking his hand, alternately staring at Dennis and her sister.

"It's so nice to finally meet you," Dennis said, giving Lauren's hand a tight squeeze. "Donald's told me so much about you."

"Really? Because he didn't tell me anything about you," Lauren said quizzically.

"Oh, and this is Sydney," Donald said, less enthusiastically.

"Ah, yes, Sydney," Dennis said, mirroring Donald's weak wave.

Sydney didn't bother to reply.

"Okay, everybody, showtime," the choir director said, clapping his hands to get everyone's attention. Clearly oblivious to the drama, he started directing the altos to the rear, the sopranos to the front, the baritones to the middle. "Let's go people!" he shouted, looking at his watch. "Let's not keep the organist waiting!"

Donald turned back to his audience, not really caring about the attention he and his "friend" were drawing. "Okay, look, Lauren, I'm going to say this only once: Go get your man and stop caring about what everybody else says about it." Just as suddenly, Donald snapped his fingers. "Or maybe you can bring him to you!"

"Donald, what the hell are you talking about?" Lauren asked, clearly confused.

"Bring him to you. You know, invite him to the party."

"What party?" Lauren asked.

"Come on, sweetie, the Thanksgiving soiree at the lake house. What party? The party I haven't gotten an invitation to yet but plan to attend anyway. That party." Donald laughed. "And speaking of which, just where the hell is my invitation?"

"Wait, how do you know about our party? We just got permission to have the party and haven't even begun to think about invitations yet, much less who to invite."

"Don't you worry about how I found out. Donald knows everything — didn't you get the memo?"

"God, Donald . . ."

"Anyway," Donald said. "Invite him to the holiday party. Let him meet everyone, get the folks used to him — spend some time."

And with that, Donald straightened his tie, smoothed down his eyebrows with a little of his spit, kissed his man, and joined the choir line.

"Lord, I love it when a plan comes together," he giggled.

5
SYDNEY

"Tell me again how the two of you are related," Rhea shouted as every male Brookhaven student lost his God-given mind at the sight of Lauren dropping her booty down to "scrub the ground" during the freestyle portion of the varsity dance squad's performance at the final football pep rally of the season.

Sydney just shook her head. "You know, I ask myself the same damn question *at least* three times a day," she replied dryly with an eye-roll.

"Not to be funny, but there are a lot of full-time strippers that would be very intimidated right about now," Carmen added as the squad collectively shook their moneymakers until the entire student body worked itself into a frenzy.

"What can I say? The girl's got gifts," Sydney offered sarcastically as the squad wrapped up their routine. Moments later, the entire Brookhaven football team came charging out to the center court of the gymnasium through a huge paper banner, and pandemonium erupted.

Distracted by the contagious energy that filled the room, the three girls momentarily forgot about Lauren's courtside antics and jumped to their feet along with the rest of the students. "Brookhaven! Brookhaven! Brookhaven!" they chanted at the top of their lungs while waving baby-blue-and-silver miniature pom-poms. Just when the noise threatened to wake the dead, Coach Wiggins strode out to the center of the floor, grabbed the mike, and started introducing the starting players by name and position.

"Girl, Jason Danden is looking H-O-T in those tight-ass-uniform pants," Rhea hissed as Jason was introduced to the audience.

"See now, I don't know about your sister, but that boy right there . . . I can just look at him and tell he's got gifts," Carmen said as she and Rhea exchanged knowing looks.

"You guys are so scandalous," Sydney replied, trying to sound as nonchalant as possible while sneaking a peek at Jason's ample package.

"Sure, like you never noticed," Rhea teased as she attempted to poke Sydney on the side. Super ticklish, Sydney

immediately doubled over to protect her most sensitive areas.
"Come on, admit it," Rhea said, reaching in again.

"Okay, okay," Sydney giggled, straightening up. "Maybe once, from a distance, I might have thought —"

"And something tells me that you'd have no problem seeing it from a distance," Carmen cut her off with another perverted innuendo. "But the real question is, what would you do with it if you got up close?"

Sydney gasped and immediately looked around to see if anyone was listening to the X-rated conversation. Seated in the coveted bleacher seats directly behind the cheerleading squad, Sydney and her girls were in a prime location to see everything happening as well as to be seen by others. Just the way Sydney liked it.

"Shoot, I'll tell you what I would do," Rhea continued devilishly, rubbing her hands together.

"Yeah, okay, you tell me and I'll be sure to tell Tim." Sydney easily flipped the script on her homegirl. "'Cause I'm not sure that will go over real well with your Mr. Starting Shortstop."

"Whatever," Rhea pouted. "Tim Collins is so not my man."

"That's not what the YRT photos of the two of you at the Gala were saying," Carmen countered with a sly grin as she moved her pumpkin-colored Chloe bag up onto the bench from between her feet.

"Damn that Web site," Rhea grumbled good-naturedly. "They stay putting folks on blast!"

"Just the scandalous ones," Carmen mused knowingly.

"All I can say is, welcome to the club," Sydney offered with a sympathetic grin. Since the breakup, Sydney could depend on an unflattering mention on the regularly updated site at least once every other day.

"I hear ya," Rhea said just as Coach Wiggins wrapped up the rally with the opening bars of the Brookhaven school song. Within moments, the entire room was singing along at the top of their lungs. As soon as the song ended, the students rushed down to center court to pile on top of the school mascot and help pump up the team for Monday night's game.

Opting to wait for the rush to die down, the girls sat back down. "Gotta say," Carmen mused as she reapplied her sparkly Lancôme Juicy Tube lip gloss, "I love the fact that we get a half day off because of the pep rally for a losing team."

"Good point," Rhea agreed, running her fingers through the new layers in her hair. "God bless football."

Sydney snorted playfully as she continued to watch the slowly thinning crowd from their perch. On the opposite side of the gym, she spotted Marcus and his boys sitting at the top of the bleachers looking very self-important as they sneered down at the excited crowd on the floor. Sydney shook her head as his favorite phrase, "Pep rallies and athletics events are entertainment for the simpleminded," ran through her head. Ironically, his hypocritical ass never missed one. On the edge of all the commotion, Jason stood laughing and talking to his co-captain, Andre Brown. Even from a distance, it was obvious how well he filled out his entire uniform. Having both boys in one place at the same time started to make Sydney feel claustrophobic. She took a deep breath to settle her nerves. "You ladies ready?" she asked as the crowd finally dispersed enough for them to make their way to the exit. Sydney really wanted to get out of the gym before the dance squad returned to the nearby bench to pick up their things.

"And willing," Carmen replied, picking up her bag.

"Is it too early for South City Kitchen?" Rhea questioned as she tucked her crisp white shirt into the high-waisted top of her Marc Jacobs jeans.

"Yes, greedy," Sydney replied sweetly. "It's only one o'clock. Can we please try to have something a little healthier for lunch?"

"What are you saying, Syd? I thought greasy fried chicken was good for me," Carmen said teasingly as she stood up and carefully stepped down to the gym floor. "Or is that only when it comes with a plate from the Waffle House?"

Sydney shook her head. "Note to self: Must get Carmen on a comedy tour immediately," she chuckled, bending over to pick up her pom-poms and simultaneously causing her oversized YSL bag to swing around and smack the person standing below in the head.

"Ouch," Dara yelped loudly, drawing the attention of her approaching fellow squad members.

"Oh, I'm so, so —" Sydney reflexively began to apologize before realizing who she'd actually hit.

"You *need* to pay more attention to the people around you," Dara snapped dramatically.

"Whatever, Dara, you know that was an accident," Carmen replied as Sydney searched for a way to get down from her seat without stepping into the middle of the half-circle of girls ogling for a view.

"I mean, you and I both already know what sleeping on the job with Marcus got you," she grinned evilly at Sydney. "Then again, maybe I should thank you for that one, huh, Syd?"

Noticeably stunned, Sydney's bottom jaw dropped open. "Do you have *no* shame?" she asked incredulously at Dara's thinly veiled implication. She instinctively looked across the room at Marcus, who was oblivious to the escalating drama.

"Like, seriously, do we all need to know you're such a dry-mouthed slut," Rhea questioned under her breath.

A low gasp escaped the crowd of wide-eyed dancers, who stood frozen in place.

Dara flipped Rhea the middle finger. Making a point to obviously glance over at Marcus, she continued addressing Sydney. "Hmm, well that's not what our boy said last —"

"Um, just what in the hell is going on here?" Lauren

demanded sharply as she pushed her way through the ring of ponytailed zombies. At the sight of her sister's ashen face and Dara's contemptuous smirk, she stepped between the two and turned to face her squad. "This ain't any damn carnival sideshow! Get your crap and hit the track. Practice starts in five minutes," she snapped. "So unless you cows want to run laps from now until the game on Monday, you better get moving!" Within seconds, the girls grabbed their duffel bags and disappeared.

Once they were all gone, Lauren faced Dara. "Um, is there a problem?"

"Nope. I said what I had to say," Dara gloated as she grabbed her stuff and headed out the door behind the rest of the squad.

Lauren rolled her eyes at Dara's retreating back before turning back to face Sydney. "Hey, I don't know what just happened, but —"

"Save it," Sydney coldly cut Lauren off. She stepped onto the floor beside Carmen and waited for Rhea to hop down, too.

"Huh? What did I do?" Lauren questioned defensively. "I don't even know what just happened between you two."

"Yes, the hell you do," Sydney spat back contemptuously. "Shoot, if I can recall correctly, you knew a long time before I did. So please don't bother trying to do something about it now, all after the fact."

"Let it go, Sydney," Carmen said softly to her friend. "It's not worth it."

"No kidding, Carmen," Lauren snipped. " 'Cause if this is what I get for trying to have her back, let me just mind my damn business." And with that, Lauren grabbed her duffel and stomped away.

I cannot believe that sloppy-ass hooker just tried me like that, Sydney thought as she sat in the front seat of Carmen's Freelander, fuming. Counting backward from ten, she exhaled loudly and turned to the backseat, where Rhea sat looking just as annoyed. "So on a scale of one to ten, how bad was that?"

"Definitely a ten," Rhea groaned as she slipped on her pink Chanel sunglasses.

"The best part," Sydney started to say as she turned around to dig her phone out of her bag, "is that, not even two days ago, Marcus was all up in my face talking about how much he missed me and wanted to get back together!"

"What?" Carmen exclaimed as she abruptly stopped backing the truck out of the parking spot and looked at Sydney like she had three heads. "And there that idiot was, all loud and proud about being with him last night!"

"Yes, ma'am," Sydney replied.

"She's crazy and he's pathetic," Rhea mumbled glaring out the window in the direction of the track.

"Negroes K-I-L-L me," Carmen said with a shake of her head as she resumed driving.

"Mmm-hmm," Sydney chimed as she finally found the slim iPhone tucked between two spiral notebooks. "But I got something for the both of them."

"What you talking about, Syd?" Rhea questioned, leaning forward between the two front seats.

"You'll see," Sydney murmured as she tapped away. Moments later she triumphantly pulled Jason Danden's contact information up and showed it to the girls.

"Oh, shoot," Carmen hooted as they pulled up to a light.

"You weren't playing when you said you had something!" Rhea exclaimed. "That boy is straight smoking."

"I can't believe I've had this number for two months and never once used it," Sydney confessed, somewhat embarrassed at her naiveté. "But you know what? It's a new ballgame now."

"Can the church get an 'Amen'?" Rhea called out, throwing her hands up like she was in the middle of a Sunday revival.

"I can't wait to see the look on Marcus's face when he sees you and Jason boo'd up all over the place," Carmen snickered. "He is so not ready for the upgrade."

"Please, the entire school is going to be looking at him like, 'You let Sydney Duke go for that chick?'" Rhea added with glee.

Sydney's iPhone rang out — it was a text from Lauren. Sydney sucked her teeth, rolled her eyes, and huffed. "I swear, my sister is going to be the death of me," she said out loud, punching the READ button to see what she wanted. Don't pay Dara any mind, she's an ass. I hate her and Marcus. Will handle. Sydney just shook her head.

"What's wrong?" Rhea inquired.

"Lauren. Trying to make nice," Sydney practically snarled.

"Ugh. So happy to be an only child," Carmen chuckled.

"Whatever — so not wasting another breath on that bull. Got bigger fish to fry. You guys can call me and Jason Barbie and Ken 2.0," Sydney joked as she pushed the CALL button and signaled to her friends to quiet down when it finally connected. After five rings, Jason's voice mail picked up. Channeling all things sexy into her voice, Sydney left a message: "Hey, Jason, it's Syd. Just thought I'd give you a call to see what you were doing after practice tonight. I know you've got the big game coming up on Monday night, but I was hoping we could hang for a little while. . . . You let me know." Sydney turned to her friends expectantly once she disconnected the call.

"You better work," Carmen hooted as she hopped around in her seat.

"Thank you, thank you very much," Sydney accepted her friend's praise with a satisfied smile.

"Well, if you ask me, an emergency trip to Gucci and the spa are in order," Rhea announced from the backseat. Already on her cell, she booked a four o'clock body treatment, massage, and mani/pedi at Spa Sydell for three. "You've got to step correct with the first impression."

"And let us not forget to stop by Neiman," Carmen said, adding her two cents. "Every new relationship deserves a fresh set of panties and bras."

"True indeed, true indeed," Sydney nodded in agreement, hoping the sexy lingerie boutique had something in purple. After all, Jason did say the color looked hot on her.

Shortly after seven o'clock, the freshly rubbed, scrubbed, painted, and waxed Sydney emerged from Sydell looking extremely unhappy. "So what do you guys think," Sydney sighed looking down at the "0 missed calls" message displayed on her phone. "Should I just call him again?"

"Hmm, I don't know, Syd," Carmen said, waving her Limo-scene pink nails gently as they waited for the attendant to pull up with her truck.

"I mean, he can't really still be at practice, can he?" she asked in disbelief.

"We could always drive back by the school and check," Rhea offered helpfully.

"I mean, I guess," Sydney said hesitantly. "But it's been

almost six hours. They wouldn't still be practicing this long. That just seems a little crazy, no?"

"Six hours is a long time," Carmen agreed as she carefully handed a tip to the attendant holding the door open for her. "I don't think going back to school is a good look."

"This is, like, so embarrassing," Sydney said as a second attendant opened the door for her and Rhea. "What if," she started dramatically, "he heard the message and was, like, forget her. Or worse, played it in the locker room for all the guys on the team to hear. I feel like such a fool." Even though, in her heart, Sydney was positive Jason wouldn't do something like that, insecurity was getting the best of her.

"Get a grip, Syd," Rhea stated as she settled into the backseat. "Jason seems like a good guy. I don't get that trifling 'Spencer from *The Hills*' vibe from him at all."

"Besides, it's not like you sent him nudie pictures or anything," Carmen added, snapping her seatbelt closed. "All you did was ask whether he was interested in hanging out."

Sydney looked down at all the bags at her feet. She felt silly for rushing out with the black AMEX before she confirmed the date. She settled back in her seat and fastened her own seatbelt. "Thank God for the small things," she replied with an ironic smile.

"Stop worrying. He's gonna call you back, Syd," Carmen reassured as she turned up T-Pain's latest single and started the car.

"And when he does, you'll have the perfect pair of purple undies," Rhea teased as she reached up front and ticked Sydney.

"Okay, okay," she giggled. "I promise, no more stressing." Dropping the phone into the empty cup holder, she put on her cherry-red Kate Spade sunglasses and chilled.

"Call me when you get home," Sydney called out as Carmen pulled around and out of her driveway. She stopped to wave at the workers on the lawn and adjusted the bags in her hands. As she started digging in her purse for the keys, her phone started to vibrate and light up. It was finally Jason.

"Hey, J," Sydney said brightly.

"Hey, Syd," he replied hesitantly. "Did I catch you at a bad time?"

"Not at all," she answered, smiling at the sound of his voice. Abandoning her search for the keys, she walked away from the front door. The last thing she wanted was to have this conversation within fifty feet of her mother's supersonic ears.

"Yeah, so I see you called earlier . . ." Jason began.

"Mmm-hmm, sure did," she said as she faced the water fountain.

"Sorry it took so long to hit you back. I offered to give a couple of teammates a ride out to Decatur after practice and it took much longer than expected," he explained.

Sydney thought about all the horrible reasons she'd created in her mind for the time lapse. Carmen and Rhea were never going to let her live her schizoid car behavior down. "It's fine. I figured you'd get around to it when you had a chance," she said nonchalantly.

"Well, I don't want you to think I was blowing you off or anything crazy like that," Jason continued.

"Not at all," Sydney said, pretending to be shocked at the idea.

"Cool, cool," he replied slowly. "So here's the thing. I really can't do much 'til next week besides eat, sleep, practice, and repeat."

"Oh," Sydney replied, immediately disappointed. Paranoia rising, she wondered whether his schedule was really that tight or if he'd seen the commotion in the gym and decided she was too much drama to deal with. "That's too bad. I was kinda hoping —"

"But, um, I mean, I can definitely give you a call when I'm free," he interjected before she could even finish her sentence.

Genuinely relieved again, Sydney happily accepted his rain check. "You know, I'd like that."

"True," Jason responded. "Me, too."

6
LAUREN

"I mean, seriously — did you see her?" Lauren asked, leaning into the full-length mirror in the dance squad clubhouse, her new groupies, Cassie Aaron and Inga Union, clinging to her every word. After the embarrassing Sydney versus Dara screaming match at the pep rally the day before, Lauren was on the warpath, and Dara, her ex-best friend, was the official enemy. It was because of that heiffa that Sydney was mad at the world again, with Lauren back out in the doghouse. Normally, Lauren wouldn't really give two buckets about Sydney's attitude, but, right about now, her sister was the only person on the earth who knew all the intel on the West End saga. So she kinda needed not to be on Syd's shit list (though she'd never admit that mess out loud). She wasn't sure if going after Dara would get Sydney to snap out of her funk, but it was worth a try. Besides, Lauren needed to get back at her for getting all flip in the lip with her in front of the squad and half the student body while she was getting her shine on.

Forget what you heard: This was Lauren's damn house, literally. Altimus had seen to it. The year before the twins made their way from Harbor Montessori Middle to Brookhaven, Altimus, at Keisha's direction, contributed $150,000 to his daughters' future school, half of which Brookhaven officials quickly dedicated to a fund created specifically to benefit the schools' cheerleading squads. The donation came with the strong "suggestion" that a building be erected in honor of the dance squad, and, of course, its generous benefactor. The wall in the clubhouse made very clear who ruled the edifice: A month before the twins began their freshman year at Brookhaven, the janitorial staff, at the direction of Brookhaven's vice chancellor and dance squad faculty advisor, painted the inside walls hot pink with light pink polka dots in Lauren's honor and hung portraits of the past dance squad captains in order of service, with a spot reserved for whichever Duke girl would be anointed dance squad captain. Lauren's picture went up in her sophomore year, smack in the center of all the others at the head of the room (double the size of all the others, of course). Shoot, the name on the façade said all anyone needed to know — it wasn't called the Duke House for nothing. Of all people, Dara should have known better than to disrespect the legacy.

So on this day, as the dance squad prepared to move the crowd at the football game against College Park High, Lauren's mission was to remind everyone, but especially Dara, just who the hell was in charge. She was going to absolutely obliterate her ex-best friend's rep at Brookhaven — so let it be said, so let it be done. Lauren dabbed some Bare Escentuals nude gloss on her bottom lip, rubbed both lips together to spread the shine, then went in for the kill. "Are 'honey blonde streaks randomly dispersed throughout jet-black Hawaiian silky-past-the-shoulder-blades' hot now? Really? Wow," Lauren said wryly to her audience. Cassie and Inga howled so hard they practically had to hold each other up.

"And her decision to pair the Catherine Malandrino knockoff mini with those nurse shoes was, um, interesting," Lauren piled on, speaking slowly to make sure the duo could give a friends-and-family encore performance of her Dara disses. "And correct me if I'm wrong, but just because the tag says 'Prada' doesn't make it so. Carrying bootleg handbags is against some kind of town ordinance in these parts, isn't it? Really, she needs to put it back in her broke-ass mama's closet, or somebody needs to call in the law, or both."

"Oh, my God," Inga said between gasps. "Stop. It. Now. I can't go on — I can do no more."

"For real, you know you wrong," Cassie added, carefully rubbing tears from her eyes so as not to disturb her freshly applied mascara and eyeliner.

"No, Dara's wrong for showing up to dance rehearsal with an unauthorized makeover a few hours before our game," Lauren snipped. "I really was about to have a Naomi Campbell, hit-a-bitch-with-a-cellphone moment, but, lucky for her, my new iPhone is acting up."

"Don't you mean your mother confiscated your iPhone? That *is* why it's 'out of service,' right?"

Lauren caught Dara's image in the mirror, connected the voice with its owner, got a firm grasp of the words that had just come out of her mouth, and then saw red. No way she was standing in the middle of Lauren's sacred domain, yelling out all her business for the world to hear and post on YRT.

"Actually, sweetie, no one was talking to you, so why don't you pick up your lip and get the hell on," Lauren sneered as she turned to face Dara. She let her eyes lumber slowly up Dara's body, from her shoes up to the top of her weave, then shook her head, gave a little chuckle, and faced the mirror again, like she was finished. But Dara wasn't about to go down that easily.

"You may not have been talking to me, but you damn sure were talking about me," Dara snipped. "But let me tell you something, Ms. Duke. People who live in glass houses shouldn't throw stones."

"Ew," Lauren said, adding a mocking shiver. "You're so . . . so . . . deep." Cassie and Inga snickered, giving Lauren even more inspiration to bury Dara. "Did you pick that up at one of your sessions at the Total Learning Concepts tutoring program you're in? Glad to see your mother's getting her money's worth."

"Look, you can try to bad-mouth me all you want, but the fact still remains that Marcus is mine now, your sister is old news, and, well, your little Boyz N the Hood fantasy is crashing and burning right before your pretty little eyes," Dara said. "How is your boo Jermaine, anyway?"

"Please," Lauren laughed, turning around. Dara flinched when Lauren took a step closer; Cassie and Inga leaned in. "You ain't nothing but Marcus's plus one — a groupie who'll be dismissed with a quickness after he finishes wearing you out. I give it, oh," Lauren looked at her TAG, "to the end of the weekend. Tops. Hope you got someone lined up. Oh, wait — there's always someone lined up for you, right, Dara?"

"I learned from the best," Dara said, albeit weakly.

"Yeah, well, um, obviously, your note taking was about as effective as it is in most of your classes. Unfortunate for you, I'm not giving remedial lessons. Now, why don't you run along, dear, get changed, and maybe pull that Hawaiian silky into a bun so you don't call so much attention to yourself while we're out on the field. *My field.*"

"Actually, I won't be cheering tonight, or any other night on this squad," Dara said. "Screw this, I quit. I don't need to be on this stupid team anyway."

"Well yeah for us!" Lauren said, punctuating the "yeah" with a rah-rah toss of her hands and a kick for good measure.

"Look for me up in the stands — I'll be sitting in Marcus's lap," she said, turning abruptly on her heels and heading for the exit.

"Tell Marcus he should use two condoms," Lauren yelled.

This time, Dara didn't bother answering back.

Lauren turned back to the mirror and checked her gloss one more time. She could hear the band lining up in the hallway, tuning up its instruments as it prepared to make its entrance. "Come on, y'all," Lauren said, switching her hips on her way toward the locker room door, Cassie and Inga hot on her trail. "It's showtime."

Lauren swore she saw her life flash before her eyes. The burly offensive lineman from College Park High was intent on not letting tight end Jason Danden make first down again, and so he did everything within his power to keep him from the 42-yard line, putting every ounce of his strength, speed, and brutishness into pancaking Jason into Brookhaven's sideline, right at the feet of the dance squad. Lauren was just finishing up a chant, bouncing around on her toes, and hyping the crowd when they piled into a heap on top of her sparkling silver Reeboks, sending both her and her pom-poms flying into several other squad members. The College Park lineman bounced up like it wasn't anything, hooting and high-fiving his fellow teammates over his victorious sack, but Lauren was clearly going to need a minute or two to get over her near-death experience.

"You okay?" Jason asked, rushing over and extending his hand to help Lauren up. Still stunned, Lauren couldn't find any words for a response, but she grabbed his hand and let him pull her to her feet. Damn — he was kind of a hottie. If she wasn't strung out on Jermaine like a crackhead, she might have had to make like a good Christian and extend the hand of fellowship to Jason in her cuddle corner at church on Sunday.

"You okay?" Jason repeated before shoving back his mouthpiece. Lauren, now surrounded by her fellow squad members swarming and clucking and dusting dirt off her knees and skirt, managed an "I'm good," before Jason rushed back onto the field, his teammates slapping his back and yelling and offering up "way to hustle."

"Ohmigod, Lauren, you almost got sacked by number ninety-five," Cassie said.

"Well, nobody said this job wasn't hazardous," Lauren offered, still a bit stunned. "I hope they at least give his ass a flag for tackling Jason out of bounds."

"Nope — *nada*," said Inga, sucking her teeth. "I swear that ref must be on College Park's payroll. He's conveniently missing all the calls and we're getting k-i-l-l-e-d out there."

"Shoot, we'd be getting slayed even if every call went our way. Brookhaven football officially sucks ass," Lauren chuckled as she grabbed her pom-poms from Cassie. "Come on, everybody — I'm all right," she insisted. "Time for the basket toss. Cassie, Inga, you guys base me."

And with swift precision, the squad lined up in three groups of four, with Lauren in the middle, smiling and happily accepting her applause from the crowd, which was on its feet and clapping for her miraculously quick comeback.

"B-R-O-O-K-H-A-V-E-N," the squad yelled as Lauren and the two other flyers were hoisted into the air. Lauren, who learned from Keisha how to concentrate and hold the attention of the crowd by focusing on one specific person in the audience, scanned the bleachers to find someone to stare at as Cassie, Inga, and another squad member, Morgan, hoisted her into the air. The field lights blared down on the bleachers, giving a spotlight effect on the crowd, which pulsed with blue-and-silver "Brookhaven Eagles" sweatshirts and flags, and painted faces contorted into angry directives for the team to "Come on!" and "Hustle, Eagles, hustle!" Somehow,

Lauren's eyes landed on a shirt that wasn't blue, perhaps because it stood out from the school colors that dominated the stands, perhaps because he was one of the few people not clapping and yelling like a maniac. This person, a young man, was wearing neon yellow — a hoodie — with an oversized gray T-shirt with a silver skull peeking from beneath. His cap was twisted to the side of his face but pulled down low, almost as if he were trying to hide behind it. But, for Lauren, that face was unmistakable.

It was Jermaine.

Lauren's heart raced as Cassie and Inga popped her into the air. She'd performed the move she was executing — a kewpie — a million times, but this minute, right now, she could barely breathe, let alone stick her jump with her man staring back at her. As she waited for the count-off that would signal her bases to pop her into a basket toss, Lauren searched Jermaine's face for a sign that he was watching her back. Their eyes connected just as Lauren pushed off Cassie's and Inga's open palms; if she wasn't mistaken, she saw a smile cross his face just as she hit the ground.

The impact made Lauren black out, if only for a second. But she quickly came to her senses — had to. What kind of mess was this, the captain of the dance squad busting her ass in front of a stadium full of people? "Seriously, I'm fine, dammit," Lauren insisted as she struggled to get up off the turf. Truthfully, her head hurt like hell, and her left knee, which was scraped and bleeding, felt like it was going to fall off her leg. But the last thing she wanted to suffer through was everybody fussing over her while she sat on her behind humiliated in front of hundreds of onlookers, who'd sent up a collective "Doh!" when Lauren missed her queue and fell directly on top of Cassie before rolling onto the ground. A few people stood up to get a closer look at Lauren mopping up the floor; still others covered their mouths and pointed as they exchanged "Did you see that?" stories with their seatmates. Lauren caught a glimpse of Dara mid-fallout, pushing on Marcus's shoulder while the two of them laughed it up. That made Lauren see red.

"Don't touch me," Lauren yelled at Cassie and Inga, whom she made a mental note to torture at the next practice. Maybe she'd make them do ten-pound arm curls for a half hour straight, so they'd have the strength next time to catch their flier before she hit the turf.

Lauren popped up on to her feet and a forced herself to do a "high V" and a "herkie jump" to signal to the crowd that it was all good, and then hopped through the squad's signature Eagles chant while she scanned the bleachers for Jermaine. But he was gone, his spot in the center thirteenth row now filled by some fool with his face painted silver and blue, screaming at the top of his lungs and waving a "Go Eagles!" flag.

* * *

He was not at the concession stand. He was not near the funnel cake booth or the Brookhaven paraphernalia tent. He wasn't by the bathrooms. Lauren pushed past the rowdy Brookhaven fans waving their flags and hooting and hollering and chanting and bumping chests like the football team had just won the Super Bowl — Brookhaven was victorious, 36 to 35 — hobbling all over the state-of-the-art football complex, looking for him under the bleachers, near the football clubhouse, and in the parking lot near her car. But Jermaine wasn't in any of those places, either. Indeed, by the time she finished searching for him, Lauren pretty much convinced herself that her eyes were playing tricks on her and that the guy in the neon yellow hoodie really wasn't Jermaine — just her wishful thinking. She hobbled back to the Duke House, anxious to nurse her swollen knee with an ice pack and then change out of her dirty uniform so she could get back home. Most of the squad had already made their way to their cars while Lauren was on her Jermaine hunt, so, thankfully, she had the locker room all to herself. Just as she hobbled up to her locker, situated right in front of the full-length mirror and flat-screen television, she heard a cell phone ring tone sound out in the quiet room. She looked around to see who might be there with her and got a little frightened for a moment as she searched for the source of the ring tone — it was D'Angelo's "Lady." Her ears led her to her own locker; she moved her towel and makeup bag and felt around the top shelf until her hand landed on the vibrating piece of metal — a KRZR with a note attached to it that said, "Answer Me." Lauren opened the phone and pushed out a tentative "Hello" that sounded more like a question than a greeting.

"I've missed you," the voice on the other end of the line said.

Lauren, who was holding her breath, exhaled and let out a tight little scream. "Jermaine? Is that you?" she asked excitedly. "Where are you?"

"Whoa, whoa, first things first," he laughed. "How's that knee?"

"Knee? What the? . . . Boy! Where are you?" Lauren demanded. "And how did you get into my locker? And whose phone is this?"

Jermaine was quiet at first. "I wish I could be right there next to you, but it's just not safe right now."

"So I hear," Lauren said under her breath.

"Lauren, look, I'll give you more details later," he continued, missing her comment completely. "But right now, I just want to make sure that you're straight. You good?"

"The best I've been in weeks." Lauren sighed. "I've been so worried about you, wondering where you are, thinking you didn't want me anymore because you didn't answer my e-mails and phone calls, and your moms has made it clear she doesn't want me to call the house. Your cell phone is disconnected."

"Yeah, I had to drop the number; it was hot. But I got a new phone, and a friends and family plan so that I could get one for you, too. Don't give the number out, okay? Think of it like our special hotline. I'll only call you, you only call me on this number, okay?

"Now look, ma, I gotta bounce, but I'm going to try to call you later on tonight, or maybe tomorrow. You should put the phone on vibrate so your pops don't know you got a phone —"

"But do you have to go? Are you around here? I can meet you —"

"No, babygirl, I already said it's not safe. Just know that we have a way to communicate now, all right? I'll hit you back."

"But —"

"Lauren," Jermaine said, cutting her off. "I love you. I'm going to see you soon."

And with that, he was gone.

7
SYDNEY

"No way," Sydney squealed into her cell as she lay across her bed flipping through the November issue of *Vanity Fair* that arrived earlier that morning.

"I'm telling you, *chica*," Rhea insisted on the other end of the line. "I was sitting in Spanish, trying to learn a little something, when everything went down! First, Dominique whispered to Elonda that a reliable source informed her that you guys were planning to ride up on white horses. Then Tristan — who you know can't stand the best bone in Dominique's little anorexic body — started getting loud about how bootleg Dominique's intel is and basically announced that you guys were already confirmed to arrive via hydroplane!"

"What in the world," Sydney exclaimed, completely flabbergasted by all the growing drama swirling around the twins' impending Lake Lanier holiday soiree. Despite the fact that there had yet to be a formal announcement made, it had become the most highly anticipated event around the Thanksgiving holiday. With exactly eighteen days left 'til the day Altimus and Keisha had designated for the girls to have their little blowout, Sydney was definitely feeling the pressure. "Okay, just so you know, *your* people are crazy!"

"Those are not my people," Rhea corrected sarcastically. "And don't blame me 'cause everyone thinks your party is about to be the location of the Second Coming of Christ."

"Not the Second Coming of the Lord," Sydney snorted as she gave up trying to concentrate on her dress hunt. Gently earmarking a Narcissco Rodriguez number, she closed the magazine. "First of all, it's really not about to be shit if Lauren and I don't get started on the planning," Sydney sighed audibly as she flipped over on her back and picked at the coral polish on her toes.

"Uh, what do you mean, 'get started,' " Rhea asked incredulously.

"Well, with everything going on, would you believe Lauren and I haven't even decided on the guest list? Or met with the planner? How crazy is that?"

"Wow," Rhea replied. "And this whole time I thought you were withholding invites to hype up the drama à la *My Super Sweet Sixteen*. You know, kinda like, My Super Hot Holiday Party . . ."

Laughing, Sydney sat up on the bed. "I wish!"

"Regardless, even if it's the freaking day before, I've heard that Renaldo is such an awesome planner, he'll get it done right. I mean, he pulled off Shar Jackson's Ultimate Revenge party within hours of Britney and K-Fed's divorce," Rhea assured. "So all I'm saying is, please just make sure I get my invite *and* the secret password. 'Cause word on YRT is that the lake house is just a front and it's really jumping off in the secret bat cave!"

"Please stop," Sydney smiled at the image of a secret sliding-rock entrance — all the better to keep certain folks, aka Dara and Marcus — the hell out.

"I'm just saying," Rhea cajoled.

"Stop or I'm telling Carm and we're both putting your butt on time-out," she threatened playfully as the sound of a bag bumping against the wall caught her attention.

"See how y'all be ganging up on me?" Rhea asked, feigning helplessness.

Standing up, Sydney headed over to her bedroom door. "Whatever," Sydney replied as she noticed the light on in Lauren's room down the hallway. "Anyhoo, looks like Lauren just got home. Let me go and try to figure out what she's trying to do."

"I'll talk to you later," Rhea promised, and hung up the phone.

Slipping into her favorite fuzzy slippers, Sydney padded softly down the hall. She hoped to catch Lauren before her Mariska Hargitay–obsessed ass got all engrossed in some TNT rerun of *Law & Order: SVU*.

"Hey, you busy?" Sydney asked as she knocked gently on the door and peered around it. She spotted Lauren on her knees, halfway under the bed, talking a mile a minute.

"Argh, I freaking hate when I drop my things behind my bed! It is so damn dusty. I swear sometimes Edwina be slacking on her cleaning game . . ." She continued unaware of Sydney standing at the door watching her Citizens for Humanity–clad booty bob up and down.

"Hey, Lauren," Sydney repeated, clearing her throat.

"Anyways, can I tell you how this whole boyfriend thing has me so crazy? I don't know if I'm coming or going. I swear, life was so much simpler before I gave a damn about anyone but my —"

"Lauren!" Sydney snapped.

The red-faced twin finally pulled her body out from under the bed and turned to face Sydney. "Um, Donald, lemme call you right back," she continued as Sydney noticed the silver house phone headset in her left ear. After a brief pause, she pushed the button and disconnected. "Why are you yelling?" she asked, slowly standing up.

"I've been standing here like a dummy trying to get your attention for the past five minutes," Sydney exaggerated.

"Okay, you got it," Lauren said, not bothering to refute the dummy description. It was obvious she was far from over Sydney's blowup at the gym.

"Listen," Sydney sighed, pulling on her favorite Victoria's Secret pink boxers, "I wanted to let you know that our planning meeting with Renaldo is on Thursday evening at seven-thirty. Since Altimus is flying him in from Los Angeles just for the meeting, you would want to make yourself available."

"I hear what you're saying, but honestly, I'm way too stressed to concentrate on a party right now. I mean, have you forgotten that my *man* is under investigation?" Lauren asked contemptuously.

"Lauren," Sydney said, struggling to remain levelheaded. "Considering our *father* is locked up as a result of the same investigation, I doubt I could forget. How-some-ever, blowing off the party will send up too many red flags. If you don't show up to the meeting, Mom will know something is up."

Lauren looked at Sydney like she was speaking a foreign language. "Fine, fine, fine, just let me think," she grumbled, pacing across the messy room. With each step, the vein in

Sydney's temple pulsated faster and harder. Finally, she came to a stop and faced Sydney. "Okay, here it is — the invitations should have my picture on it, I'm wearing a gold Carmen Marc Valvo dress, so naturally everything should complement that, if push comes to shove I'll do without the red carpet entrance, but Goldfinger must DJ the party," she said, ticking off her list of demands in a single breath. "You got all that? Think you can handle it from there?"

Before Sydney could close her gaping mouth, the phone started to ring. She clicked the earpiece. "Hello? Wait, what?" Lauren questioned the caller incredulously before throwing her head back in laughter. When she eventually pulled herself together, she turned to Sydney, mouthed the phrase "Please close the door on your way out," and used the TV remote to turn on *Law & Order*.

"What I'm envisioning is . . . snow. Lots and lots of snow! Maybe an igloo with a blizzard," Renaldo announced dramatically after sitting with his eyes closed and his fingers on his temples for what felt like hours to Sydney.

"Snow?" she asked in disbelief. "Um, Renaldo, sweetie, we're in Georgia. Southerners don't do blizzards," Sydney said as gently as possible considering all she wanted to do was slap some sense into his crazy artistic head. After two (torturous) hours, three glasses of wine (his), and countless ideas (horrible), the *über*-fabulous Renaldo and a very frustrated Sydney were no closer to figuring out what the hell the theme of the twins' ultimate holiday bash was than Sydney was to forgiving Dara. Granted, it didn't help matters that Sydney's brain was still burning from her sister's diva moment the other afternoon. Every time Sydney looked at the list that Lauren had handed her this morning — comprised solely of people that she *didn't* want to see at the party — she completely lost her train of thought.

"Humph, that's a very good point," he agreed, taking another long sip. Suddenly, Renaldo scrunched up his over-tanned face like he was on the verge of a major breakthrough or taking a huge dump. "I've got it!"

"Is that so?" Sydney said as she turned to accept a plate of sliced fruit from Edwina and gave her a subtle signal not to serve Renaldo another drop of wine.

"Holiday in HOT-lanta," he exclaimed, looking at her expectantly.

"I'm sorry?" Sydney asked as she looked down at her lime-green Chanel cuff.

"Get it? Hot. Red and gold everywhere, all guests required to wear red or gold!" he exclaimed, jumping to his wobbly feet. "Oh, yes, yes, yes. I can see it now! A red carpet entrance, gold candles everywhere, red signature drinks, and of course big black men covered in gold spray . . ."

Sydney almost choked on her bite of pineapple. "Excuse me?" she coughed.

Renaldo laughed at the horrified expression on her face. "Oh, I'm just teasing you, dah-ling," he said with a dismissive wave.

"Uh, okay," Sydney said, allowing a smile to cross her face as she imagined what Altimus would do to the effeminate little white man if he even thought there would be naked black men at his daughters' party.

"But seriously, what do you think? If you like, I can definitely work it out, no worries," he assured confidently as he finally stopped sipping and started scribbling in his notebook.

After giving it some thought, Sydney shook her head affirmatively. " You know, Renaldo, I believe I can see the vision. . . . Wait! What about the invitations? We're only two weeks away and the invitations haven't gone out yet."

"Oh, I know," Renaldo clapped his hands gleefully. "You and your sister can tape a video invite! I actually had Ray J do one for the release of his duet album with Lil' Kim and it was too many things!"

"You know, to be honest, I'm not so sold on anything Lil' Kim is doing these days," she replied, trying to be as diplomatic as possible. "Not to mention, good luck trying to get Lauren and I together to make that. We might do better with something more realistic like singing invitations from the last round of *American Idol* castoffs," Sydney joked bitterly as her cell phone vibrated. Looking down, she read the new text message: Come thru, u've got mail. Aunt L.

Less than fifteen minutes later, the car service pulled up to the Duke house to take Renaldo and his promises of "the best holiday party Atlanta has ever seen" back to Los Angeles on the first thing smoking. And Sydney, under the guise of a crucial last-minute school assignment, was on her way across town to her Aunt Lorraine's house.

Even though she was sure no one under the sun besides Aunt Lorraine knew where she was headed, Sydney's heartbeat raced as she pulled her car onto I-85. "We been too strong for too long, and I can't be without you bay-bay," she sang along with Mary J, pressing the accelerator well beyond the 65 mph speed limit. It'd been a little over a month since Dice's arrest and subsequent re-incarceration. Since then, aside from the occasional update from Aunt Lorraine, Sydney hadn't heard anything from her father.

As Sydney finally pulled her car up to the dilapidated little house's driveway, she could barely breathe. "Calm down, Sydney, calm down," she muttered, pulling down the visor to do a quick check on her windblown tresses. Screwing up her face, she made a mental note to schedule an appointment for a blowout first thing in the morning. Now that she no longer had Marcus's controlling ass breathing down her neck about keeping it natural, she was looking forward to trying out some new hairstyles.

Just as she was about to open the car door, her phone vibrated again. "Oh, shoot," she muttered, praying that it wasn't Keisha calling her on her bluff and demanding she come home right now. She made a quick sign of the cross and clicked the pink Bluetooth she still had in her ear.

"Hello," she answered hesitantly.

"Hey, Syd, what's up," a friendly voice with just enough bass to be neither Keisha nor Altimus responded. Sydney's whole body relaxed in relief.

"I'm good thanks. . . . Um, who am I speaking with?" she asked

"You can relax, it's Jason," he laughed as she exhaled a loud sigh of relief. "Dang, your caller ID on the fritz or have you erased my number already?"

"Whatever," Sydney retorted as a smile spread across her face. "My phone is at the bottom of my bag so I answered the earpiece without looking at the caller ID." Although they'd traded a couple of brief text messages since the game, for the most part the two had played phone tag, making this their first real conversation.

"So what's up with you? Where you at? You sound like I caught you in the middle of something," Jason asked innocently.

"I-um-I'm-" Sydney started to stutter as she looked around at her surroundings. Realizing there was no way she could tell the truth, she struggled to come up with something believable that wouldn't lead to more questions. "I actually just came out to my car to grab a notebook," she finally responded.

"Oh, okay, true. So you're still studying, huh?"

"Um, yeah, I'm still studying," Sydney replied, noticing movement behind the drapes in her aunt's living room window. She knew she needed to get off the phone before Aunt Lorraine came outside and called her out. "So what's up," she asked, getting to the point.

Seeming a little thrown off by her straightforward attitude, Jason began slowly. "Well, you know, I told you that I would give you a call after the game. . . ."

"Mmm-hmm, you sure did," she said, trying to encourage him to get to the point.

"Although, I wasn't sure if you were going to wanna speak to me after what happened at the game with your sister and all," he joked nervously. "I damn near knocked her out."

"Oh, no, I should probably be thanking you," Sydney insisted, realizing that he was probably taking her tone the wrong way. "I can't even count how many times I've wished someone would lay Lauren's smart butt out," Sydney said, throwing in a cute giggle.

"Well, in that case, I'm happy I could help," Jason responded, finally loosening up. "I was just thinking, maybe this Saturday night, if you're not busy —"

"Saturday night is great," she enthused before he could even finish his sentence. "Why, Jason, I'd be delighted."

"True," he replied simply. "Well, I guess I can —"

"Just text me the details during the week." She cut him off abruptly.

"Uh, okay, that works."

"Wonderful. Now lemme go," Sydney stated, bringing the conversation to an end just as the front door started to open. "I'll see you tomorrow, J!" she offered, and hung up before he even had a chance to say good-bye.

Sydney turned on her car alarm just as Aunt Lorraine swung open the creaking screen door that barely hung on to the doorframe by one and a half hinges. "Well, if it isn't my favorite richy rich niece," Aunt Lorraine drawled. "Your stuck-up mama buy you that pretty bracelet or was it some boy?" she asked sarcastically of the bright cuff bracelet that still adorned Sydney's wrist. Wearing a dingy housecoat over a pair of washed-out pink pajamas, a head full of rollers, and a pair of flip-flops, she looked like a caricature of the stereotypical ghetto welfare mom.

"Hey, Aunt Lorraine, I got your text," Sydney replied, choosing to ignore her aunt's smart comments as she walked up the uneven pavement of the walkway.

"I see," she snickered, holding the door for Sydney so she could enter the dimly lit foyer. "You best be careful driving too fast in that shiny car of yours. I don't know about how it is ova' by where you stay but 'round here the cops arrest first and ask questions last. Ya heard?"

"Yes, ma'am," Sydney answered respectfully, looking around the cluttered space. The tattered couch where she had spent several afternoons visiting with her father when he was out on parole was now covered with laundry. Piles of old newspapers stood in the corner. She shifted uncomfortably in her Tory Burch leopard-print ballet flats.

"You want something to drink? I got some red Kool-Aid in the fridge," her aunt offered gruffly as she headed into the tiny kitchen. Sydney watched as she lit her cigarette on the flame from the gas stove's left burner.

"I, um, actually, kinda have to go," Sydney started, secretly relieved that she wouldn't have to be in the claustrophobia-inducing space with her sour-faced aunt much longer. "I told my mom that I was running to the library to study. . . ."

"Well, don't let me keep you, Cinderella, -ella, -ella," Aunt Lorraine quipped as she pulled two letters out of the pocket of her housecoat. "I wouldn't want your car to turn into a pumpkin or nothing." Sydney chuckled uncomfortably as she turned the letters over in her hands and looked at her father's familiar chicken scratch handwriting. The sense of déjà vu was overwhelming.

"Thanks, Aunt Lorraine, this really means a lot," Sydney offered sincerely as she tucked the letters in her black Hermes Kelly bag.

"Mmm-hmm, don't mention it. And let's just hope that them worthless detectives hurry up and catch whoever the hell killed that ole knucklehead, Rodney Watson," she said with a slight cough. " Or you're going to be right back picking up letters again for the next fifteen years, minimum."

"Excuse me?" Sydney asked incredulously as the meaning of the words *minimum* and *fifteen* refused to register. "Are you saying my father is facing fifteen years?"

"Uh-huh, fifteen *minimum*," Aunt Lorraine confirmed as she took a deep drag and exhaled through her nostrils. "Welcome to the real state of Georgia, princess."

8
LAUREN

Altimus was going to be at the dealership all day and late into the evening, and Keisha, never one to rest easy in her solitude, claimed she needed some face-time with the girls, so she booked a suite at Le Madeleine Hotel and arranged a "Luxe Girls' Spa Day" for three, with all the trimmings. If only for a moment, Lauren thought it was odd that they'd be getting another rubdown just a week after Keisha had sprung for the massage and facial that, unbeknownst to her mother, she'd skipped out on. But, well, it wasn't Lauren's stilo to question, particularly when an herb-infused, detoxifying body wrap and spa lunch was involved. Besides, after both of her near-death experiences at the football game Monday night, she needed someone to lay hands on her aching back and sore knee, even if she had to suffer through an afternoon with Keisha and Sydney, who, even on a good day, had become a little hard for Lauren to handle.

Before Keisha could even close the heavy front door, Lauren took off for the massive mahogany writing desk, which was decked out with a welcome arrangement of all their favorites: a heap of chocolate-covered strawberries for Lauren, sparkling cider and apple-cinnamon PowerBars for Sydney, and champagne, of course, for Keisha. Lauren grabbed a berry and twirled herself onto the sofa, grabbing the remote with one quick motion.

"God, please, can we have just one afternoon without the television blasting?" snapped Sydney. She eyed the apple-cinnamon PowerBar and let her fingers linger over the cider, then settled on a bottled water before walking over to the window. They had a perfect view of the lake, which was wrapped in a panoply of fall orange, red, and yellow trees making their slow, serene march into winter. Quietly, Sydney was looking forward to a little R & R to help calm her nerves for her big date with Jason, but nobody really needed to know all of that. "This is supposed to be a day of relaxation. Can't we just be quiet and enjoy?"

Lauren sucked her teeth. "I can't think of a better way to relax than zoning out to one of my favorite shows. If it's complete silence you're looking for, I'm sure it's nice and quiet in the lounge area down at the spa. Help yourself to an early start," Lauren huffed, pointing to the door and pushing the ON button on the remote all at once.

"Are you freakin' kidding me? I don't have to go —"

Keisha cut Sydney off. "Have mercy, this is supposed to be a friendly girls' day out," she said, loud enough to make both the girls jump. She squared her shoulders, poured herself a glass of bubbly, and started giving orders. "Both of you go in the bedrooms and change into your robes. We have about thirty minutes before our massages and body wraps, and I want to get down to the lounge area to have a few more sips of champagne and read my *Essence* before our appointments begin. And I would prefer not to have to go down there with all this chitter-chatter ringing in my damn ears."

"Sorry, Mom," Sydney offered quickly. She put the top back on her bottled water and made her way over to the bedroom. Lauren didn't say a word — just kept flipping through the channel guide, looking for an old episode of *Law & Order: SVU*.

Keisha eyeballed her daughter and shouted, "Lauren! I said come on!"

Lauren slowly turned off the television and headed for the basket of candy strawberries. She took a bite, then waltzed up to her mother and gave her a sloppy, chocolate-covered kiss. "Thanks for the spa date, Keish. You're the one."

Keisha chuckled and shook her head as she watched her daughter prance into the bedroom, but her smile vanished as quickly as Lauren disappeared. She took a sip of her champagne and swallowed hard, her eyes focused on the door long after it closed.

"This treatment originated in seventeenth-century Indonesia," the masseuse practically whispered as she poured the fragrant drink into Keisha, Sydney, and Lauren's teacups. "It was a purifying ritual performed on Javanese princesses on the night before their weddings. First, you'll sip this infusion of warm water and ancient herbs, which will help your muscles release toxins. . . ."

Lauren took a sip of the tea and almost threw up. Honestly, she wished the woman would shut up and get to it already. Sydney, who was clinging to the masseuse's every word, was wearing the hell out of the goody-two-shoes thing, and Lauren, who was never, ever in the mood for dissertations, especially didn't want a two-hour lecture on Indonesian royalty and old herbs and what was about to happen to her; she just wanted to get up on a table in her own private massage suite and get her rub on.

"We'll follow your full body, aromatic hot-oil massage with a deep-penetrating mask, followed by an invigorating scrub and a private steam shower. You'll then be invited to soak in a sea of rose petals in our luxury bath, which —"

"Ugh. Can you take this tea? It's nasty," Lauren demanded, cutting off the woman. She held up her cup as if it was a rogue, stinky sock. Sydney tossed Lauren a look so cold it could have solved the global-warming situation, but Lauren didn't give a damn. Of course, neither did Keisha. After all, Lauren had learned the art of demanding servitude from the best: her mother.

"Oh, sure thing," the woman stammered, taking the cup from Lauren's hands.

"Can you show me to my room? I'm ready for my princess massage," Lauren said, standing and letting her robe fall open enough to give her breasts a little Beyoncé jiggle.

"Well, um," the woman stammered again, this time facing Keisha. "You don't have a separate room; we've arranged for a three-way massage, as requested by Mrs. Duke."

Lauren, confused, pulled her robe tight around her neck and tossed a "what the hell" look at her sister, who had the identical quizzical look on her face.

"A three-way?" Sydney asked, frowning. "How's that going to work?"

Keisha sucked her teeth. "Simple. She's going to show us to the room where they've set up three tables side-by-side so that we can chat while we get our rubdowns," she said. She turned toward the tea lady and asked in a firm voice, "Where's the room?"

"Uh, yes, yes, Mrs. Duke — it's right this way," she

directed, her hands outspread toward a double-door suite just down the hallway. "I'll go fetch Jade, Lisa, and Beth directly so that you may begin your massages."

"Uh-huh, thanks," Keisha said, tossing her chin in the direction of her girls. "Let's go."

In a jif, the three were in the room. Sydney and Lauren were still dumbstruck by Keisha's decision to include them in her own normally private spa appointment, and secretly disappointed that they wouldn't have complete and utter quiet while they enjoyed their massages. Each disrobed in silence, wondering what, exactly, was so damn important that it had to be said over the din of the classical music, which, if the masseuse was worth his or her salt, usually put Lauren to sleep. A nap is what she wanted; Keisha's voice was not.

"See, isn't this nice, girls? The three of us here, enjoying one another's company?" Keisha said. If the girls were listening closely, they would have heard the slight hint of sarcasm in her voice.

"Yeah, lovely," Sydney said.

"Swell," Lauren added.

"Come on, girls — it's not often you and your mother get to sit and enjoy one another. Every mother should get to enjoy her daughters, don't you think?" she asked.

"Oh, no, you're right, Mom," Sydney said as her masseuse rubbed her hands vigorously to warm the oils. "This is nice."

"Yeah, you know I don't mind spoiling my babies," Keisha said. "You may be seventeen and looking grown, but you're still my babies. And I would do anything for you."

God, shut up already, Lauren said to herself, wishing she could say it out loud.

"But I won't tolerate any disrespect, you know what I'm saying?" Keisha asked, her voice growing dark. "I was raised to know that children have their place — you know, 'Don't speak unless spoken to'? 'Do what I say'? My personal favorite was 'Stay outta grown folks' business.' Lord, my mama sure did believe in that one, hard and strong."

Lauren's ears perked up; she knew something wasn't right.

"That's why I invited the two of you here today, to give you a review of all the lessons I've learned over the years — particularly my favorite one," Keisha continued, her voice slightly muffled as her massage therapist dug into her shoulders, forcing her head deeper into the pillow cradling her face. "Stay outta grown folks' business. Simple concept. Easy to do. But for some strange reason, y'all act as if it just doesn't apply to you. So I'm here to set it straight. It does."

"Mommy, what are you —" Sydney began.

"Oh, no, sweetie, it's Mommy's turn to talk, your turn to l-i-s-t-e-n. Isn't that what Beyoncé and them said? 'Listen,'" she sang off-key. "Oh, wait, though, my jam was that Keisha Cole song, 'Let it go, let it go, let it go,'" she continued to sing. "Yeah, nice strong messages in them there songs. Listen, and let it go. Both of you should try it."

The smell of ylang-ylang and vanilla wafted into Lauren's nostrils, a quick reminder that she was not dreaming. Her mother was really in the massage suite at Le Madeleine, bugging the hell out of her and laying down messages about as sinister as an Abu Ghraib CIA interrogation. If the masseuse wasn't pushing down on her back so hard, and she wasn't afraid that her mother would slap it back down, Lauren would have lifted her head to get Sydney's attention. Instead, she lay silent. Still, she could hear Sydney's breathing over the music.

"Your father — Altimus, not the scumbag I had two babies with — has done nothing but be good to you, love you. Every stitch of clothing you have on your backs, every piece of leather you have on the pretty little feet you use to push the gas pedals in the cars you drive, every expensive handbag you dangle from your dainty little arms? Altimus bought those. Not Dice. Not Lorraine. Not Jermaine. Not any of those bastards. That's all Altimus up in your closets and in your driveway and in your wallets," she said sweetly. "You better recognize."

"Mom, what are you talking about?" Sydney said, putting on her best syrupy voice. "Of course we appreciate everything Dad's done for us —"

"Sydney, save the bullshit for somebody else," Keisha

snapped, knocking her masseuse back as she sat upright. "And I don't recall asking either one of y'all to say anything. For once, just listen. I hired somebody, did you know that?" she continued just as forcefully, waving off poor little Beth, who didn't know what to do or say now that she was caught up in Hurricane Keisha. Keisha didn't pay her a lick of mind. "Yeah, my friend is a sweet little guy from back in my days in the West End. Yeah, knows our old stomping grounds real good. Buckhead, too. Has the cutest little gift of knowing just how to blend in, so he can see but not be seen."

Keisha let that hang in the air a minute. There wasn't so much as a peep out of her daughters. The masseuses working on the girls tossed ole Beth a look of sympathy and dug into the girls' backs, if only because they didn't know what else to do while their clients received their custom cuss-out.

"My friend has been checking into things for me ever since I realized somebody's been rummaging through my old boxes downstairs. Oh, he's had a great time watching my little girls run all around the West End, trying to dig up dirt on folks. He cracks me up trying to keep track of who's who. I keep telling him, the twin who dresses like she's straight out of a Ralph Lauren catalogue is Sydney; the one who dresses like I would if I was a rich seventeen-year-old from Buckhead is Lauren. After that, he was straight, but I would have been able to tell who was who just by who went where anyway," she said.

Sydney visibly shivered. Lauren opened her eyes and stared at the floor, steeling herself for an ass-kicking. She just knew it was coming. She wondered which one of the heiffas at the last spa dropped dime on her, even after tucking her crisp fifty-dollar bills in their bras. She said a silent "fuck me" to herself and waited for the ax to fall.

"I'll bet Aunt Lorraine was only too happy to tell you a bunch of bullshit about Altimus and me, huh, Sydney? Old hag — never could mind her damn business."

"But I didn't —" Sydney started.

"Girl, I know you not gonna lay there and tell me some stories — not here, not now. Don't you know who I am?" Keisha said through her teeth. She didn't give Sydney a chance to reply — not that Sydney didn't know better at this point to shut her trap. "Now this is going to be the last time I say it, hear? Sydney. Stay the hell away from Aunt Lorraine. For real, for real. She don't know shit about Altimus, or me, or what we all got bubbling. Keep your ass out of the West End and forget about Dice. He ain't shit, ain't never been shit, ain't evah gonna be shit, and ain't nothing you can do to change that."

"Excuse me," Beth interrupted. "I'll just step out for a minute and —"

"Uh-uh, where you going?" Keisha yelled. "You ain't finished here. I paid my money — strong, green money — and you gonna give me my dollar's worth. Now stand right there. I'll let you know when I'm ready."

Beth didn't move, and the other masseuses practically stopped breathing, as did Sydney and Lauren. Keisha got up from her table and started pacing the marble floor of the room, running her fingers over the oils and hot stones on the small table that held the massage supplies.

"Stay away from Aunt Lorraine and Dice. And stay the hell out of my things," Keisha demanded, practically snarling the words in Sydney's ear. Sydney, mortified, couldn't stop shivering. "That's my stuff down in the basement, and you don't have any right rummaging through it like a little rat.

"And, Lauren?" she continued.

Oh, shit, here it comes, Lauren said to herself, girding her shoulders against the masseuse's hands. She considered stuttering something, but she thought better of it.

"Not only do you need to stay out of grown folks' business, you need to keep your business off the damn Internet, especially if you're trying to hide the fact that you've been trying to get in touch with that little thug from the SWATS. You should take his advice and give him space," Keisha said, walking slowly over to Lauren's table. Lauren was steeling herself for Keisha to bring up her daughter's impromptu Jermaine hunt last Saturday, but it didn't come up. Neither did, thankfully, Jermaine's visit to the game Monday nor the phone she'd secretly stashed in her purse. "Make that a permanent space, hear me?" Keisha continued. "Just because his brother got stomped out on his front lawn doesn't mean you have any business running in the streets after him. Have some pride — stop playing with yourself. And stop playing with me. I told you to stay away, Lauren. Stay away."

"O-okay," Lauren stuttered.

"I'm not playing with you, Lauren. Ain't no good gonna come out of it if you keep digging into that mess. It ain't none of your concern. Go find one of those cute little boys on the football team. Hell, get back with Donald, for all I care. No Jermainc.

"Oh, and Sydney, one more thing, dear," Keisha said sweetly. "So what Marcus dipped out on you — get over it. I already went to too much trouble ensuring his political future by contributing too much money to his mother's political campaigns to throw away this relationship. All men got flaws, little girl, and Marcus ain't no different. Dog him out a little bit, make him buy you something nice, and then get back to it, already.

"Now," Keisha huffed as she lay back on the massage table. "Beth? Let's get it done, baby. Come on, all this stress got Mama a little tight all up in the back area. Can you work that out?"

"Uh, yes, um, yes, Mrs. Duke," Beth said, hopping to attention like someone pushed her in her back.

"Great." And then to Lauren and Sydney: "Oh, and remember: What I said in this room stays in this room, hear me?" Keisha warned. "And I expect that we won't have to take any more girls' spa days for this reason. I don't need this damn aggravation."

And with that, Keisha put her head into the massage pillow and didn't say another word for the rest of the treatments, except "May I have another" to anyone standing within ten feet of a champagne bottle. Lauren and Sydney? Well they were quiet, too.

9
SYDNEY

"Sooooo, are you ready?" Carmen and Rhea simultaneously burst out as they excitedly pushed their way into Sydney's bedroom and almost toppled to the floor.

Sydney stuck her head out of the bathroom, where she was fighting with her hair, and pouted, "No! Do I look ready to you?" Turning back to the huge mirror over the "his and her" sink top, she slammed her brush down dramatically. "I have been trying to do something with my hair for the past hour and it just won't cooperate. I freaking give up," she announced, and stormed out to join her girlfriends.

"Humph, you better figure it out, princess; it's already seven-thirty," Rhea said, doling out the tough love as she hung her green Dior saddlebag on the back of the desk chair and picked up the copy of *Vogue* laying next to Sydney's laptop. She headed over to the bed and sat down to flip through the pages.

"Rhea! Don't be such a bitch!" Carmen admonished playfully as Sydney stuck out her tongue. Walking over to Sydney, she put her arms around her best friend's shoulder and gently led her back into the bathroom. "Relax, Syd, it's not as bad as you think. Just let me help you with it," she offered kindly.

"Thank you for at least trying to help a sista out, Carm," Sydney tossed over her shoulder as the two disappeared into the bathroom.

"I am trying to help," Rhea replied with a grin over the top of the magazine. "By keeping your slow butt on schedule."

"Yeah, yeah, yeah," Sydney retorted playfully as Carmen worked on her head. "With friends like you, who needs enemies?"

"Mmm-hmm, whatever," Rhea said as she finished flipping through the pages and rolled over onto her back. "So have you figured out how to explain Jason to your parents?" she asked as she watched the slowly rotating ceiling fan. " 'Cause I know Keisha Duke is not going to be happy about the changing of the guard."

"Oh, she made it very clear that she was not having it," Sydney responded cryptically. She winced from the pain of Carmen twisting her hair into a dramatic chignon. "Ouch!"

"Oh, stop being so tender-headed," Carmen mumbled around the hairpins in her mouth.

"Wait, how did your mom even find out? You didn't tell us you told her! When did you break the news that you and Marcus broke up?" Rhea asked sitting straight up on the bed in shock.

Realizing that she may have said too much, Sydney faked a cough to buy herself some time to think. "Um," she said clearing her throat, "I guess Lauren must have let it slip or something . . . I'm not really sure." She tried to keep a straight face and gently pulled on her right earlobe.

Carmen shook her head disappointedly. "Your sister never ceases to amaze me," she said, finishing Sydney's 'do with a spray of olive oil sheen.

"Aww, Carm it's perfect! Thank you so much," Sydney exclaimed as she turned to give her girl a big hug. "If that doctor thing doesn't work out, you should definitely look into beauty school," she teased as she continued to admire herself in the mirror.

"I'll keep that in mind," Carmen laughed as she put the oil sheen down and stepped back and held up a small handheld mirror so that Sydney could see the back.

Rhea popped her head in the door. "Let me see," she

demanded. Sydney turned and modeled her fabulous new upsweep that, thanks to a couple of perfectly placed loose curls, was just the right balance of casual and sexy. "Oh, wow, we like," she co-signed emphatically.

"Now if you can just help me decide what to wear . . ." Sydney whined again.

"Uh-uh, that's your department, Rhea," Carmen teased as she playfully passed Sydney along to Rhea. "I've done my part for the cause."

With an exaggerated roll of the eyes, Rhea grabbed Sydney by the hand and led her out of the bathroom and into her enormous walk-in closet. "Come, my child," she said in an authoritative voice. "Together, we will find you the perfect 'Beware: Horny sex goddess hidden beneath this good girl façade' outfit for your little rendezvous with Mr. Danden," she joked. Carmen burst out laughing as she followed behind the two.

"Whatever you say, Andre Leon Talley, Jr.; just don't have me looking like J-Hud at the MTV Awards," Sydney retorted.

"Eww, that above-the-knee gold lamé was the absolute worst!" Carmen screeched as they collectively remembered the time the normally impeccable Dreamgirl made a huge fashion misstep at a most important award show.

"Give me a little credit," Rhea insisted as she slowly circled the perimeter of the closet, picking out various items along the way.

Carmen looked at her pearl-face Rolex. "T-minus thirty-five minutes 'til the doorbell rings . . ."

"Actually, I'm going to meet him at the movie theater," Sydney hedged, immediately looking away.

"Excuse me? Rhea stopped dead in her tracks and looked at Sydney.

"Um, since when do we meet our dates in the street?" Carmen inquired disdainfully.

"Well, what had happened," Sydney started. "Since, um, Lauren, um, spilled the beans to Keisha, I couldn't really get away with faking like Jason and I were strictly hanging out as friends —"

"Oh, I get it," Rhea interjected as she brought over a pair of black skinny jeans, plain long-sleeve black T-shirt, and hot pink Michael Kors kimono-sleeve jacket. "Here you go," she said, handing the outfit to Sydney. "This with the suede and waterskin Jimmy platforms that you bought last weekend."

"Hot to death," Carmen co-signed with a nod.

A mischievous grin spread across Sydney's face. "Jason has no idea," she said slyly.

"None," Rhea seconded as she headed to the door. "Come on, Carm, let me show you the dress I think I want to wear to the holiday party while Syd gets dressed and puts on her makeup." As Carmen followed behind Rhea, she paused to throw a thumbs-up sign at Sydney.

About fifteen minutes later, Sydney stepped out of the bathroom with her outfit and makeup done. "Wow," both girls said in awe.

"I'm thinking these diamond hoops that Marcus gave me for Valentine's Day last year," Sydney said as she held up one earring to her lobe for them to examine.

"Works for me," Carmen said.

"Perfect. Then I think I'm ready to go," Sydney said, turning to grab her silver LV doctor bag.

"I just have one question," Rhea said, raising her hand as if she were in class. "How are you planning to get past Keisha looking like that?"

"Mmm, good point, Rhea," Carmen concurred as she pulled a pack of Big Red out of her black Gucci fanny pack and passed out pieces.

"Oh, I'm good. I told you how obsessed my mom has become with HGTV lately, right?" The girls nodded in response. "Well, now she's decided that she wants to take interior decorating classes."

"Okay . . ." Rhea said looking unclear.

"Well, her classes are normally on Wednesday nights. But this week her instructor got called in at the last minute to appear on a Rachel Ray special and canceled class. The makeup class just so happens to be tonight," Sydney finished up with a triumphant grin. "By the time she gets home —"

"You'll be long gone!" Rhea exclaimed as she high-fived Sydney.

"There is a God," Carmen said with a smile.

"Wait, what about Altimus?"

"Honestly, I don't think he's home from the dealership. He's been working really late nights recently," Sydney mused as she took her cell off the charger and tossed it in her bag.

"Hmm, well let's get the hell out of here before he comes home," Carmen said, walking over to the closed door. Rhea grabbed her bag and followed behind Carmen. "You ready, Syd?" she questioned over her shoulder as she gave Carmen a nudge to hurry and turn the knob.

"I'm about to," Carmen complained as she finally opened the door. And faced Altimus.

"Good evening, ladies," he stated simply as the two struggled to contain their gasps.

"Sir," Carmen replied with eyes as wide as saucers.

"Good evening, Mr. Duke," Rhea replied as she turned back to look at Sydney, who was frozen in her tracks.

"Uh, hey, Altimus," Sydney stuttered. "What's up?"

"Nothing. I was hoping to have a word with you before you went out for the evening." He looked at Carmen and Rhea pointedly.

"Um, we'll catch up with you later, Sydney," Rhea said as she pushed Carmen out the door.

"Yeah, Syd, we'll call you," Carmen offered over her shoulder as the two hurried down the long hallway.

Without so much as a backward glance, Altimus stepped in the bedroom. "You got a moment?" he asked as Sydney started pulling at the diamond hoop.

"Um, yeah, sure," Sydney said, turning away. She looked at her watch. She had exactly three minutes to get out of there or she was going to be late. "What's up?"

"Well, first of all, I feel like we haven't spoken in a really long time. How's school? What's up with your classes? I hope we're still on track for that scholarship to Brown," he joked as he sat down on her bed.

"Um, sure," Sydney hedged. The last thing she wanted to do was get into a detailed conversation about school. Aside from the time factor, nowadays she was barely keeping up in the classes she used to kick butt in. "You know, everything is good. I've just been really swamped with preparing for the SATs, volunteering at the shelter, planning our holiday party at the lake house, and whatnot . . ."

"True. You look very nice. Got big plans for tonight?"

"No, not really," Sydney said, stalling for time by walking over to the bed and picking up the magazine. As she put it back on her desk, she debated using Marcus as an alibi but changed her mind at the last second. "Actually, I'm going with a couple of kids from my French class to see this foreign film that's playing at The High."

"Hmm, okay. Well, I'm glad to see you're getting out." Altimus said thoughtfully, " 'cause your mom told me that you and Marcus broke up."

"She did," Sydney gasped, shocked that her mother shared information she clearly obtained from her private investigator. Then again, after the day she'd just had at the spa she knew better than to put absolutely anything past Keisha Duke.

"Yeah, she called me on her way to class and said that you mentioned it while you girls were spending time at the spa today," he said.

"Is that so?" Sydney asked, trying not to roll her eyes at Keisha's blatant lie.

"I hope you're not mad that she told me," Altimus said as he reached to touch her arm gently. Sydney recoiled at his touch. "I could tell she didn't think the breakup was a very good idea, huh?"

"Are you surprised?" Sydney asked sarcastically, folding her arms across her chest. "Sometimes I think she loves Marcus more than me. . . ."

"That's a bit much," he chuckled, looking at the copy of *Vogue* Rhea had left on the bed.

"Whatever," Sydney mumbled as she looked at her nails.

"Regardless, I just want to let you know that as much as I liked Marcus Green, I love you," Altimus continued, walking over to where she was standing and lifting her chin so he could establish eye-to-eye contact. "And it's his loss to suffer silently. But if he or *any* guy you're dating ever gets out of line, I will not hesitate to make them sorely regret it for a very long time," he stated definitively in a very low voice. "Because no one messes with my mine."

By the time Sydney rushed into the lobby of the theater, she was twenty-five minutes late and a hundred percent stressed out. Struggling to catch her breath from the run over from the parking lot in her stiletto boots, she anxiously looked around for Jason. *Damn, I hope he didn't leave*, Sydney worried as she looked guiltily at her watch. Chewing nervously on her bottom lip, she pulled out her phone and called Jason's number. It went to voice mail. Sydney decided to walk around slowly. "Please, please, please," she muttered to herself with every step. About to give up, she spotted a very familiar figure wearing a bright yellow Izod shirt, dark blue Red Monkey jeans, bright white Air Force Ones, and a worn fitted Yankees hat, leaned up against the wall. A huge grin of relief spread across her face as she adjusted her outfit and headed over.

Walking up directly behind him, Sydney tapped him on the shoulder. "Hey, you," she said sweetly, trying to sound adorable. However, when Jason actually turned around to face her, all the cuteness drained out of Sydney's body.

"There you are," Jason exclaimed as he stepped aside to reveal his very condescending-looking ex-girlfriend, Tyra Edwards, right behind him.

"Hey," she offered, giving Sydney the official cut-eye.

Realizing the awkwardness of the moment, Jason jump-started the introductions. "Sydney, this is Tyra," he said, pointing to each girl respectively. "And, T, this is my um, friend, Sydney."

"Nice to meet you," Sydney finally squeezed out.

"Mmm-hmm, I'm sure," she replied dismissively. "Well, it was really good to see you, J," Tyra said to Jason as she reached up to give him a lingering kiss on the cheek. "Promise to come down to FAMU whenever you schedule your HBCU college tour. We'll have *so* much fun."

"No doubt," he responded with an uncomfortable smile.

"Great. And don't forget to give your parents my love," she tossed over her shoulder as she sauntered away, shaking her butt extra hard.

After an extended moment, Sydney cleared her throat and spoke stiffly. "I feel like I interrupted your little reunion. . . ."

"No, no," Jason reassured as he pulled the brim further down on his hat. "Not at all. I literally just ran into her a couple of minutes before you got here."

"Is that so?" Sydney asked, trying to suppress the sarcasm.

"Yeah, I guess she's home for the weekend. Tomorrow is her baby sister's birthday, so she came to spend time," he explained.

"That's nice of her. Did she invite you to the birthday party?" Sydney asked, spontaneously, not sure whether he would be offended by the question and become defensive.

"Oh, naw," he responded easily. "It was a nice surprise to see her, but I'm not the kinda guy who believes in sending mixed signals. If we ain't together like that, I don't need to be hanging out with her fam' at the private celebrations. You know what I'm saying?"

Sydney released a small, silent sigh of relief. "I hear ya," she said, thrilled that he had all the right answers. "So is it too late to catch our movie?"

"You know, I actually got the starting time wrong," Jason said, pulling the tickets out of his back pocket to look at them. "Showtime starts at nine-thirty not nine-fifteen, so we're good."

"Great," Sydney enthused. "I've actually been dying to see this movie for the longest."

"Me, too," he replied casually, putting his arm around her shoulder and leading Sydney into the theater.

* * *

"Okay, that was so good," Sydney exclaimed as the flow of the crowd pulled them along and down the escalator toward the exit.

"I know! How crazy was the scene where they were slap boxing on the wing of a moving Lear jet?" Jason questioned as he gestured wildly like a little kid. Sydney giggled softly just watching him.

"What?" he asked when he realized that she wasn't laughing at his description of Jackie Chan.

"Nothing," Sydney said with a smile as she spontaneously reached up and gave him a quick kiss on the cheek. "You're just really cute when you're excited about something."

Jason took her hand softly and said, "Then I guess I'm always going to be cute when I'm with you."

"I sure hope so," Sydney said softly as she drew small circles in his palm.

The escalator finally reached the bottom floor and the couple strolled toward the exit doors. "So what do you feel like eating?" Jason asked.

"Hmm, I'm not sure . . ." Sydney started, and then stopped mid-sentence. The only word she could use to describe the sight of Marcus opening the door for Dara was "Wow." Marcus stopped cold when he finally looked up from Dara's cleavage and saw Sydney standing with Jason Danden.

"Sydney, what are you doing here?" he questioned defensively, looking at Jason like he wanted to kill him dead.

"I would ask you the same, but it's all so clear now," Sydney hissed back as she cut her eyes to Dara, who appeared unnaturally bloated in her gray Rock & Republic jeans and Ed Hardy long-sleeve T-shirt.

Forgetting about Dara, Marcus stepped to Jason. "I don't believe we've met. I'm Marcus Green, Sydney's boyfriend of the past four years."

"Hmm, well thank God for the future, right, Syd?" Jason smirked. And without missing a beat, the two walked out the door and into the night hand-in-hand.

10
LAUREN

"So repeat it back to me because we know how you do," Lauren whispered into her recently recovered iPhone as she snuggled under her massive triple-down comforter. She scratched her scalp through the wilted-silk night scarf that held her wrap in place, and made a mental note to call Jamila, her hairstylist, for an appointment, seeing that her hair was a straight wreck. About this, she was not happy, because she'd have only about forty minutes after her parents headed off to church to shower, dress, put on her makeup, and get her hair to look like something other than a rat's ass before Jermaine got to the house. She may have been skipping her weekly gathering at the Lord's house to get her reunion on with her man, but that wasn't about to stop her from having a little talk with Jesus in hopes he would help a sistah get it together.

"I got you," Donald practically yelled into the phone. "I mean damn, you said it five times, I said it four times, so unless you changed some of the details without making it plain between the last time I ran through them and now, do I really need to repeat it again?"

"Yes, dammit," Lauren huffed, snuggling into her pillow as she put her best friend through the paces of how to keep her parents on the road while she entertained Jermaine. "I want you to be absolutely sure about —" she started. Her heart practically jumped out of her chest when she heard footsteps coming down the hall. "Hold on!" she said quickly before stashing her cell under the oversized Brookhaven Prep dance squad teddy bear propped up against her headboard. She watched the doorknob to her bedroom turn and tried not to let her eyes go wide as saucers when her mother peeked her head in.

"We're about to head to church," said Keisha, her wide-brim church hat tottering against the doorjamb. "Edwina already left for chapel, but she left some pancakes and bacon in the warmer for you."

"Thanks, Mom," Lauren said sweetly, trying her best to hold it together. "Honestly, I think I'm going to take some Aleve and go back to sleep. Maybe by the time I wake up, my leg will feel better and this killer headache will have gone away," she added, rubbing her head for added effect.

"You'll be fine, I'm sure," Keisha said curtly. "See you in a little while."

Hopefully, longer than that, Lauren said to herself. "Have a good service," she said out loud as her mother closed the door. Only when she heard Keisha inform Sydney she had five minutes to meet her in the kitchen did she dig her iPhone out from under the teddy bear and start whispering into it again. "This is serious, Donald. Now, I need you to go over the plan one more time, because if you mess this up, Keisha and Altimus are going to drown me and my man right in the driveway fountain."

"Okay, okay. In the car on the way to church, I'm going to bring your mom's name up and remind my mom that it's been a while since we had brunch with the Dukes. Then I'm going to convince her that she should invite Keisha out after church, and I'm going to suggest we all go to Bassano's."

"And when she says Bassano's is too crowded and she would prefer to go to the Teacup?" Lauren urged.

"I'm going to tell her that I heard that the Teacup had some rodent issues and had to be temporarily shut down for a massive cleaning," Donald sighed.

"And?"

"And that I really have a taste for Bassano's French toast, seeing as I haven't had it since Daddy sent me away to Chicago. And then I'll search out Keisha as soon as we get to church and make sure she and my mother connect, so she doesn't get distracted and ask someone else to brunch."

"And then when you get to Bassano's, you'll send your plate back at least two times, and you'll take teeny-tiny bites, so that —"

"We stay for at least two hours — I know, I know already. Don't you have to get dressed for your Sunday morning date, you big heathen?"

"Yes, I do, which is why I'm hanging up now," Lauren laughed.

"Well, don't do anything that I wouldn't do, Miss Thing."

"That certainly leaves me open to a whole lot, doesn't it, Mr. Thing?" Lauren asked back.

"Yup — sure does!" Donald laughed. "Have some good, clean, naughty Sunday fun!" Donald yelled, and hung up.

Lauren slung her legs over the side of her bed and waited until she heard one of the four automatic garage doors creak up. She tiptoed over to her window to watch Altimus pull the Mercedes SL around the circular driveway and then high-tailed it to her closet to pull together what easily could have been a three-hour hair, makeup, and wardrobe session into only a little more than a half hour. The pressure. She could hardly believe that she would finally see Jermaine face-to-face after he'd spent weeks ducking her. She still couldn't understand why he'd insisted on not answering her phone calls, texts, and IMs before he gave her the secret phone, but he promised last night that he would "break it down so it will forever be broke."

"See? There you go quoting 'love jones' again. Do you have any original lines?" she whispered into their private phone the night before, long after everyone in the house had shut off their TVs and slathered on their cold cream and said their good nights.

"I got plenty," Jermaine said. "I just wish I didn't have to tell them to you over the phone."

"Me, too," Lauren sighed. "I would give anything to have you here lying next to me. I want to feel your arms wrapped around me, feel your breath on my face."

"I know, me, too. But it's just not safe, Lauren," Jermaine said. "I've been over it in my mind a thousand times, and I just can't figure out how to see you without someone catching us — me."

"Come here!" Lauren said.

"What?" Jermaine asked, incredulous. "You want me to walk right into the belly of the beast?"

"That's why it's a brilliant plan, don't you see?" she asked. "My family goes to church every Sunday. I'll just fake like I can't make it this week. So while they're out, you're in. Nobody would expect you to have the balls to walk up into the crib!"

Jermaine thought about it for a moment, and, despite that

everything within his being was telling him this was a bad idea, he finally agreed. "What time?" he asked.

"They leave at seven-thirty for the eight A.M. service, and they don't usually get back until about ten or so. And since tomorrow is a first Sunday, they'll even have to stick around a little longer for communion."

"I don't know," Jermaine hedged. "What about your sister? Are you sure she's going to go? And just how you gonna get out of going with them? And what about the neighbors? How am I going to get to the front door without anybody seeing me? It just seems risky, Lauren, and that's my ass if we get caught."

"Let me worry about your ass and all that other stuff, too, okay? I need to see you. Come here. Take MARTA and come in through the back door at eight-fifteen, no earlier. I'll take care of everything else."

His image appeared in her mirror, just over her left shoulder, as she was putting the last bobby pin into the messy bun she was pulling together. Sheer terror crossed Lauren's face; she screamed so loud she was sure the neighbors, if they were home, would have heard her. Jermaine, thrown off by her scream, jumped and yelled, "Oh, shit — what?"

Lauren spun around. Her frightened eyes instantly smiled when she realized the strange man who appeared in her mirror was her man. "Ohmigod, you scared the mess out of me!"

she squealed, jumping into his arms and squeezing him really tight.

"You told me to come in the back door. I walked through the house, heard something up here, and figured it was you," Jermaine said, accepting her embrace.

"I just wasn't expecting you to come up is all — no biggie," Lauren gushed. "I'm so glad you're finally here."

He pulled back from her arms and took her face in his hands. "Look at you, Lauren. You're so beautiful. God, I've missed you," he said, leaning in and kissing her lips once, then twice, then again and again. Lauren put her arms around his neck and got into it, slightly parting her lips to accept his tongue. He tasted like wintergreen breath mints. She loved wintergreen breath mints.

"I've missed you, too," she said, between hugs and smooches. "Don't ever stay away from me that long again," she admonished.

"It's not like I had a choice," Jermaine said, stepping back and leaning against the bathroom wall. "Your pops? He got a brotha on the run, on the real."

"Jermaine, you just got here, and I haven't seen you in almost a month. I don't want to talk about my father or what's happened or what might be going on. I just want you," Lauren said, walking close to him and rubbing her body against his. "We don't have a lot of time. . . ."

"That's exactly why we need to talk, Lauren. We don't

have a lot of time, and there are some things you need to understand and understand quickly."

"Can't we save the serious talk for the phone?" Lauren asked, pouting. "I just want us to enjoy each other."

"Lauren, I feel you. But your pops, man, he got me trippin'."

"Which one?" Lauren asked.

"What do you mean which one?" Jermaine asked as Lauren pulled him into her room and gently sat him down on her bed.

"Which one of my fathers got you all twisted out? Altimus or Dice?"

"Why would I be scared of Dice?" Jermaine asked, frowning.

"Well, he *is* in prison under suspicion of having killed your brother, isn't he? And for violating his parole?" Lauren said quizzically.

"Hold up. You really think your father is responsible for this, not your stepfather?" Jermaine asked.

"Well, I don't really consider Dice my father — I prefer to think of him as the sperm donor who got lucky with ole Keisha," Lauren said, half laughing.

"Damn, you know less than I thought — or maybe more, I can't figure out which," Jermaine said, standing up. He rubbed his hair with both hands and walked toward Lauren's window. "Damn."

"What?" Lauren said.

"Listen to me. You need to know that Altimus Duke is not to be played with," Jermaine demanded, perhaps more forcefully than he intended.

"I think I know a lot more about Altimus Duke than you think," Lauren snapped. *God, this wasn't how this was supposed to go*, she said to herself. The plan she wanted to stick to was the one where he held her in his arms, told her how much he missed her, and they smooched and cuddled and stuff. She wished he would stay on subject.

"Look," he said. "I didn't mean to snap at you, Lauren. It's just that there's a lot of stuff happening that you don't know about, and the block is hot around my way."

"Then why don't you tell me what's going on, so that we both know what's up?" Lauren huffed.

Jermaine sighed and shook his head. "It's just that up until now, I was sure they had the wrong guy in jail. I mean, he and my brother didn't exactly get along, but —"

"Hold up. How did Dice know Rodney, anyway?"

"They were in the pen together, and had some kind of dealings once the both of them got out. But I thought they were mostly friendly visits," Jermaine said, rubbing his temples.

"Well, is there anything you've heard that would make you think differently about their relationship?" Lauren asked.

"You're his child," Jermaine said simply.

"And?" Lauren huffed. "I'm Altimus's child, too."

"Tell me about it!" Jermaine said. "I haven't heard anything but how I need to lay low because of your daddy. Yo, on the real? Altimus is a hood figure with connections that run real deep."

"Don't get it twisted. Dice is no angel and, quite frankly, I wouldn't be surprised if he had something to do with all of this," Lauren said, rolling her eyes.

"Yeah, well, as much as you may think Dice is involved, I believe Altimus knows what's up." Jermaine said.

"Why are you the one doing all the investigating, anyway?" Lauren asked, turning his face toward hers. "Isn't that what the police are for? Why not let them sort it all out? I don't understand why you have to be all twisted up in it."

"It was my brother, Lauren," Jermaine said, standing up from the bed and walking toward the window. "It would be nice to sit around waiting for the police to do their job, but it don't go down like that in the SWATS. If anybody knows anything, they damn for sure ain't telling the police, and if something happens to your people, you handle it yourself. I don't know exactly why my brother got beat down on our front lawn, but I get the feeling that it has something to do with you and me. And until I get to the truth, I can't stop."

Lauren was quiet. And then: "I met someone last week who told me you were in serious danger."

"That's the general consensus around my way," Jermaine said, half laughing.

"But I'm thinking this person may be able to help us figure this all out," Lauren said. "Maybe. He's my uncle."

"Damn, L, I'm already running away from both your daddies, you gonna bring your uncle up into it?" Jermaine huffed.

"Calm down, damn. Hear me out," Lauren insisted. "I met him last week when I came to the West End looking for you."

"Yo, you gotta stay out of the West End, for real —"

"Shh!" Lauren said, putting her finger to her lips. "Just listen. I have a good feeling about him. He actually saved me from the beat-down your girl Brandi was ready to deliver."

"Brandi, huh?" Jermaine said, recalling Lauren's earlier run-in with his homegirl, who was forever trying to hook up with him.

"Uh, yeah. We'll have to sidebar on her role in the Jermaine saga, but right now, let's focus on Uncle Larry. I don't know what it is about him, but he seemed like he might know a little somethin', somethin'. I also felt like he might be willing to help."

"Willing to help, huh?"

"Yeah," Lauren continued. "Like maybe we should try to hook up with him to get the info or advice we need to get on with it."

"I don't know, Lauren. I mean, my brother's dead, they got my moms all shook, I'm looking over my shoulder all hours of the day and night, lying low, wondering if someone's going to come get me, or the police, or who will get to me first —"

"Can we please talk about something else?" Lauren begged abruptly, turning his face to hers. "I only have you to myself for a few hours, and I've been waiting for this — for you to be standing in front of me — for way too long to be talking about this now. We're going to figure out what happened to your brother. And if either of my fathers had anything to do with his death, we're going to figure that part out, too. Trust, we're going to get to the bottom of this. But let's figure it out another time," she said, turning his face toward hers. She kissed his lips softly once, and then again, and again. He responded in kind, pulling her close to his body, their breathing bodies, their beating hearts, moving as one. After their tongues did their slow, hot dance, Jermaine pulled back and placed her hands in his. He looked over at her bed, and then she did, too. And together, they walked slowly toward it.

"Wait," Lauren said suddenly, pulling away from him and walking toward her stereo system. "I made a mix on my iPod for you. It's mostly old school stuff, Jodeci, Stevie Wonder, Mary J. Blige, and what not. But each one of the songs means something to me, and every last one of them reminds me of you," she continued as she pushed a few buttons. Stevie's "Visions" blasted through the speakers.

"You ain't got no Soulja Boy up in there? No Fitty? T-Pain?" Jermaine laughed.

Lauren was a little stunned.

"I'm just kidding," he said, pulling Lauren onto his lap.

"See? You know you wrong," Lauren giggled. "Come here," she said, tapping her lips with her pointer finger.

They kissed passionately, their soft moans going unheard over the din of Stevie's piano. Lauren used her palms to slowly lay Jermaine across her bed, then laid on top of him, squishing her body against his. She wriggled a little when his hands slid up her thigh and under her skirt, his palms cupping her butt.

If not for all that moaning and Stevie's song and the preoccupation with the hugging and kissing and rubbing, one of them might have heard the short but reasonably loud alarm that sounds when someone walks through one of the several doors leading into the Duke estate. One of them might have even heard the keys hit the ornate circular table in the foyer. Or one of them might have heard the creaking of Lauren's door as it opened.

Jermaine saw her first.

Lauren heard the gasp.

She lifted her head just in time enough to see her twin flee — down the stairs she went, two by two.

Lauren jumped off Jermaine and ran after Sydney, calling out to her like her very life depended on it. Truth be told, it did. She needed Sydney to keep her trap shut about what she saw, lest she and her man end up on the obit page of the *Atlanta Journal-Constitution*. "Syd, wait up!" Lauren yelled again, she, too, taking the steps two by two, Jermaine on her heels. The two of them burst through the glass door and pushed the heavy iron gate open.

"I forgot my notes for my meeting — I have to go," Sydney called out, shutting the car door to their father's Mercedes, which she'd apparently borrowed to double-back from church.

"Just wait, Syd, let me explain."

"No, no explanations, Lauren," Sydney snapped. "You probably ought to consider getting your boyfriend back in the house, though, before the neighbors see him. Or maybe Mom's nosy friend?"

Lauren hadn't considered the nosy friend. In fact, so excited was she about seeing Jermaine, she had forgotten that Keisha had them all tapped out like the damn FBI. Instinctively, her eyes darted wildly, looking for signs of someone in the bushes, or peeking over the massive brick fence surrounding the property, or the surveillance cameras that stood sentry over the Duke estate.

Lauren looked at Jermaine and dropped her eyes. "You better go," she said simply.

11
SYDNEY

"Okay, for the record, I so heart Jason," Carmen playfully swooned as Sydney showed her the text message Jason had sent during her last period. Attached to it was a video of a dancing teddy bear holding a sign that read: THINKING ABOUT YOU.

"I have to admit, he's really adorable," Sydney gushed, tapping back her reply as the two strolled through the outdoor courtyard full of students enjoying the sunny afternoon.

"So when are you guys going to make it official?" Carmen asked impatiently as she waved across the large atrium at a group of girls from her drama class. "I'm, like, dying to go on a double date!"

"Uh, Carm, we just went on our first date two days ago," Sydney reminded her friend as she stopped to check the pile of books in her arm for her chemistry workbook. "Can we please have a little time to get to know each other before sending out the wedding invitations?"

"Whatever, smart aleck," Carmen retorted as she waited patiently. "Aren't you the one who told me not to play hard to get when I met Michael?"

"Yes." Sydney reluctantly copped to the charge.

"Well then? Girl, you're the only one who's going to be mad if someone else makes a move on him. You see how scandalous these desperate hoochies can be," Carmen hinted none too subtly as they resumed walking.

"No, I hear you," Sydney agreed with her friend. "I just want to take my time, is all. Once word gets out, every damn body is going to be up in the business. I just want to enjoy getting to know Jason without reading about the two of us on YRT just yet."

"Good point . . . I mean seriously, damn Barbie and Ken, you guys are totally about to become Brookhaven's Brad and Angelina. . . . *Sans* the babies of course."

Sydney laughed and shook her head, imagining herself and Jason on the run from the paparazzi with a multinational brood in tow. "Yes, definitely *sans* the kids." She stopped to open the double doors that led back into the school.

As they stepped through the doors and into the building, Carmen shivered slightly under her purple-and-white

Thomas Pink button-up shirt. "Damn, why didn't I grab my wrap when we stopped at my locker," she complained.

"Umm-hmm, and you know the library is going to be even worse," Sydney mused, thankful for the lightweight cashmere cardigan she decided to wear that day.

"Hold up, Syd," a familiar voice called out from behind the girls.

Sydney turned into the crowd of students. "Lauren," she responded hesitantly.

The crowd finally parted and Lauren stepped forward. "Hey, Carmen. Um, Syd, can I talk to you for a minute?"

"Hey," Carmen replied flatly.

"Um, sure . . . Carm, can I catch up with you in a minute?"

"Sure. I'm actually going to run back to my locker, grab my wrap. I'll meet you back here later," she responded. "See you later, Lauren," she offered, heading back out the doors.

"So what's up?" Sydney asked, trying to keep things light. As a general rule, the girls hardly ever spoke in school. Not to mention, the two had been avoiding each other like cold sores on prom night since the Jermaine debacle on Sunday.

"Can we find somewhere a bit more private?" Lauren asked, indicating the library.

"Sure," Sydney said, leading the way to the individual soundproof reading rooms in the back.

"Damn, how'd you find out about these spots," Lauren asked as she dropped her vintage Louis Vuitton duffel handbag on the desk and looked around the small room that came equipped with a desk, two chairs, laptop, and flat screen TV.

"If you spent a little more time in the library, you might know about them, too," Sydney answered mockingly as she pulled a couple of peppermints out of her Bottega bag and offered Lauren one.

"Whatever," Lauren said simply as she accepted the candy.

"So, what's up?" Sydney asked, settling back in her chair.

"Okay, so obviously Keisha is not playing around." Lauren started with the least debatable topic of conversation, popping the peppermint into her mouth.

"No kidding," Sydney agreed bitterly. "That spa day shit? Like, whose mother hires a private investigator to spy on her kids?"

"I know, I know," Lauren concurred with a shake of her head. " I feel like I'm in the middle of a damn Jason Bourne movie or some shit."

"And what's so bad is, she knew every damn thing. She knew about the photo album, me going to see Aunt Lorraine, you trying to keep in touch with Jermaine. Shoot, she even knew about my damn breakup with Marcus," Sydney exclaimed.

"It's crazy," Lauren replied.

"And don't you think it's so bizarre how protective she is of Altimus? Like she didn't even bother to try and figure out what all the snooping we're doing is for."

"It is . . . but maybe she's just embarrassed that we know about her hooking up with Dice's best friend," Lauren offered with a shrug. "It is kinda sleazy . . ."

"True. But still . . ."

"I'll tell you one thing. I'm scared to take a damn dump now without Keisha running a medical report on my intestines," Lauren joked sarcastically.

"Shut up, Lauren," Sydney laughed.

"What? What did I say?" Lauren feigned mock innocence as the twins shared their first laugh in a very long time.

"I swear, some days I don't know whose egg you came from," Sydney giggled.

"Um, excuse you, that would be my egg that you came from, thank you very much," Lauren immediately countered with a grin.

"Yeah, yeah, yeah . . ."

"But seriously, Syd," Lauren said soberly. "There is one thing that Mom and Altimus don't know about."

Sensing the shift in tone, Sydney straightened up. "What are you talking about?"

"I probably should have told you this before but . . ." Lauren mumbled, pulling at a tiny ship anchor on her gold charm bracelet.

"Lauren Duke, if you don't spill!"

"Okay, so remember about two weeks ago when I went to the spa with Mom?"

"Yeah . . ."

"Well, even though I went, I didn't exactly *stay* at the spa," Lauren explained.

"You're losing me," Sydney said. "You went but you didn't stay?"

"Well, when Mom and I split up for our treatments, I kinda snuck out of the spa and went down to this fried-fish joint in the West End looking for Jermaine," she finally spilled.

"You what?" Sydney asked incredulously. "Lauren, are you crazy?"

"Sydney, I had to," Lauren whined. "Jermaine had been ignoring the IMs and the text messages I tried sending from the computer lab, I didn't know what the hell was going on, I was scared! I had to find him and make sure that he was okay," she insisted.

Crossing her arms, Sydney shook her head. "You're incorrigible," she stated.

"I know, I know," Lauren continued. "And I'm not even going to tell you how when I got down there I almost got into a fight with one of those funky ghetto bitches he used to deal with. Or at least that's what she was trying to make it seem like."

"Lauren, were you really about to get into a fight, in the hood, over some dude?" Sydney questioned her twin sister incredulously. "Seriously?"

"That's just how much I love him," Lauren answered simply.

Sydney looked down at her black Chanel ballet slippers as she remembered the surge of pure anger she felt when she saw Marcus walking with Caroline and Trina in the parking lot. "I feel ya," she replied quietly.

"So anyway, what I was about to say was that right as me and Boom-quisha were about to go to blows, Uncle Larry snatched my ass up," she continued.

"Who's Uncle Larry?"

"Mom's *brother*," Lauren paused dramatically.

"Wha — what," Sydney stuttered.

"That's exactly what I said," Lauren said as one of the cell phones in her bag started buzzing. She pulled out the KRZR, read the I Luv U text, and put it back.

Sydney looked at her suspiciously. "Um, when the hell did you buy that old-school flip phone?"

Exhaling loudly, Lauren shook her head. "That, my dear, is a whole other story. Let me finish telling you about Uncle Larry first."

"Okay," Sydney said, completely flabbergasted by all the intel her sister had managed to withhold for so long.

"So anyway, apparently he's Mom's only brother," she started again. "His name is Laurence and I'm actually named after him," she continued proudly.

"But why would we not know him?"

"I can't call it," Lauren admitted. "According to him, they were all really tight back in the day — him, her, Dice, and Altimus. Hence, the whole naming me Lauren thing. But from what I can guess, when Dice got sent away, some shit happened. And Mom just stopped dealing with him and anybody else she didn't like completely."

"Or maybe he just wasn't feeling the whole 'hooking up with your baby's father's best friend' thing," Sydney surmised sourly. Lauren shrugged her shoulders in response. "But even still," she continued, "how did *you* know to look for him?"

"I didn't," Lauren answered truthfully. "Like I said, I was in the West End, in this little fried-fish spot called Pride, when me and homegirl were about to get into it. At the last second, he snatched my ass up outta there."

"Whoa," Sydney said.

"Did I mention that everybody up in there but me seemed to already know he was related to us?"

"Kinda like everyone but us also knew that Altimus was shady," Sydney muttered sarcastically.

"But wait, it gets worse," Lauren responded as she flipped her hair over her left shoulder. "So after he drags me out the joint — and I finally stop thinking that I'm being kidnapped — he says something real crazy about how I should stay out the hood and let Altimus *and* Keisha clean up the mess they made."

"Huh? Mess?"

"Yeah, it was real weird. That and how neither me nor Jermaine is safe. Which I totally thought was some over-exaggeration scare topic until I finally talked to Jermaine face-to-face the other day at the house —"

"Speaking of which." Sydney seized the opportunity to interrupt. "I wasn't going to say anything until you brought it up, but all that Romeo and Juliet, star-crossed lovers business in the house? I hear you on the love thing and all, but ain't no love in the world saving you from becoming Atlanta's next senseless tragedy if Mom or Altimus ever, ever, ever found out Jermaine was up in the house. Let alone, in your room. I don't want to get my butt kicked trying to save your life, either. So let's not repeat that stunt again, okay?"

"Oh, trust, not even if I wanted to," Lauren said with a sly grin. "Jermaine swears he was going to piss in his pants before I realized that it was just you."

Sydney shook her head and cringed as the image of her

sister straddling Jermaine flashed through her mind. "Tell him the feeling is mutual," she replied.

"But like I was saying, Jermaine made it so clear that his life would be in danger until he or the cops figure out who the hell killed his brother!"

"Holy shit," Sydney whispered. "This just keeps getting worse and worse. Like for real, for real, I don't know what the hell we're in the middle of. Last week Tuesday, I snuck over to Aunt Lorraine's house."

"Wait, I thought you met with the planner last Tuesday."

"Guess you aren't the only one with a few tricks up her sleeve." Sydney laughed bitterly at Lauren's look of surprise. "Anyway, so Aunt Lorraine texted me — thank God Keisha doesn't have the common sense to read the incoming text message numbers on the bill — to let me know Dad sent a letter."

Mimicking her sister, Lauren crossed her arms and shook her head. "And you talk about me?" she asked.

"Whatever. And as I'm picking it up, she tells me that Dad is easily looking at fifteen more years if he's convicted."

"What?" Lauren gasped, genuinely horrified.

"I know," Sydney responded sadly.

"But- but-" Lauren stuttered. "Syd, I know I've been super skeptical this whole time, but after talking to Uncle Larry and now Jermaine . . . I just don't think he did it."

Sydney shrugged her shoulders helplessly. "Welcome to the club," she said. "But it's like, our intuition against their word. We'd look crazy trying to go to the police to report our parents." Lauren inhaled deeply as tears formed in the corner of her eyes.

Sydney reached out to rub her sister's back. "Don't cry, Lauren, okay?"

"I'm just so frustrated and confused," she sniffled as she put her head down into her hands. "This is not how my life is supposed to be turning out!"

"I hear ya . . ." Sydney agreed as her cell phone started buzzing. She pulled it out quickly. "Hello? Gimme five minutes and I'm on my way," she responded before hanging up. "That was Carmen. She's been waiting for me upstairs."

"Oh, okay," Lauren said, wiping her eyes. "I guess I should probably get going, too," she replied, grabbing her compact out of her bag and powdering her face.

"Wait," Sydney said as she stood up. "Now, what's the deal with that phone?"

"Jermaine gave it to me," she admitted with a small smile. "He knew I couldn't talk to him on the one Altimus pays for, so he got me another one on his new line."

"That was really smart," Sydney said as she pushed in her chair and waited for Lauren to finish reapplying her lip gloss.

Lauren looked at Sydney for confirmation on her makeup.

Sydney gave her a nod. "He's really a great guy . . ." she mused, fluffing her hair. She stopped suddenly. "Speaking of which, what's the deal with you and Jason Danden? I overheard Dara whispering something smart about you two when I walked in to the cafeteria the other day."

Sydney blushed and looked down at her favorite David Yurman ring. "Oh, yeah . . . we've kinda been hanging out," she hedged.

"Aw, shucks!" Lauren exclaimed loudly. "My prissy sister landed her the superjock of the year? Woo-hoo! You better work!"

Laughing at Lauren's little cheer, Sydney bashfully tried to downplay the situation. "I don't know about all that. But we did go to the movies Saturday night."

"After Keisha threatened you within an inch of your life for breaking up with Marcus, you still found the time to sneak out and hook up with another boy?" Lauren asked in awe. "Damn, maybe we really are related after all!"

"Whatever, I was not 'hooking up' with anybody," Sydney corrected. "We went to the movies and that's all."

"Mmm-hmm, sure you did," Lauren teased. "Fine ass Jason? I'll let you tell it, Syd."

"But you know, we did run into your girl Dara up in there . . . uh, looking a little puffy I might add," Sydney said as she moved toward the door.

"Eww, what the hell was she doing there?" Lauren demanded, making a screwface.

"Seeing a movie, I assume. But let's just say she wasn't alone," Sydney said, giving her a look as she opened the door and allowed Lauren to walk through.

"Humph, and that's why I cursed her fat ass out after the pep rally the other day," Lauren mumbled. "She needs to spend more time on a treadmill and less in the movies."

"Well, whatever, I'm not studying either of the two of them anymore," Sydney said diplomatically. "I don't need the additional negative energy in my life."

"I know that's right," Lauren whispered as they started to slowly walk back to the front of the library. "So I assume you're inviting Jason to the party, then."

Sydney nodded her head. "Yeah, I'm thinking if everything keeps going well between us, that'll be our coming-out moment."

"Must be nice to be able to come out," Lauren replied wistfully.

Sydney stopped and put her hand on her twin's shoulder. "If you want to invite Jermaine, go ahead. I'm totally fine with it," she suggested. "In fact, I'll lobby extra hard with Altimus to let us have a parent-free party. I'm pretty sure he'll do it if I ask . . . as hard as he's trying to get our father-daughter relationship back the way it used to be."

Lauren's face lit up like a Christmas tree. "Really? You'd do that for me?"

"No prob," Sydney replied as Lauren spontaneously gave her a hug and kiss.

"You're the best, Syd," Lauren whispered excitedly as she whipped out the new phone and immediately sent Jermaine a text. Sydney smiled as she wiped the face of her phone with the bottom of her sweater. "Okay, let's go," Lauren said as she finished. "You know I have to totally rethink my outfit now that he's going to be there."

"Just don't forget our theme — red and gold only! I did not waste hours with the crazy drunk planner for you to go left on us!" Sydney threatened playfully.

"Okay, okay," Lauren cringed slightly. "PS, my bad about bailing on all the planning. I know, I was really being a lot . . ." she offered meekly.

Sydney rolled her eyes and smiled. "Don't even worry about it. You and I got bigger things to worry about. Besides, what do they say, you can't pick your family?"

"Kiss my butt, Sydney Duke," Lauren said, relieved to be off the hook.

"I'll let Jermaine handle that, my dear," Sydney teased as they stopped beside a large concrete pillar.

"You shut up," Lauren retorted a little too loudly for the likes of the unhappy-looking librarian sitting at the nearby front desk. "Anyhoo," she continued loudly just to be difficult, "I am totally psyched about our little soiree now . . ."

"Yeah, crazy how we can even get excited about this with all the drama going on, right?" Sydney whispered extra low trying to make up for Lauren. "Although I have to admit, if Renaldo pulls off all the crazy stunts he keeps dreaming up, it's going to fabulous."

"Humph, and you know I believes in a dream —" Lauren started.

"Me, too," Marcus said suddenly, appearing from the other side of the pillar and staring directly at Sydney. Both girls froze in place.

Recovering faster than her sister, Lauren sneered, "Er, um, I don't remember anyone inviting you or your patchouli stink into our conversation, Rasta Boy!"

"Whatever, Lauren," Marcus continued dismissively. "I'd like to speak with Syd."

"She's not interested in anything you have to say," Lauren snapped, but this time Sydney put a restraining hand on her arm.

"It's cool, sis, I got this," she said gently.

"Okay, if you say so," Lauren said uncertainly. "But I wouldn't get too close. I heard hair ticks just jump from head to head if you're not careful," she said, looking disgustedly at Marcus's hair before she turned on her Marc Jacobs boot heel and bounced.

Acutely aware of all the prying eyes surrounding them, Sydney turned and whispered, "Marcus, this isn't the time or place."

"I know, I know," he pleaded. "But things are getting ridiculous. Now, you're at the movies with that bighead jock —"

"Let us not forget that you were there your damn self with fat ass Dara," Sydney hissed as she turned and started walking up the steps to the upper level.

"Fine, you're right. I was," Marcus whispered as he followed behind her. "So we're both with the wrong people. Now what?"

"The problem is, Marcus, I don't think Jason is the one that's the wrong person for me," Sydney said as she reached the top of the landing and looked around for Carmen.

Marcus grabbed Sydney's arm. "Fine. You've moved on. I'll accept that. But can we at least figure out how we can save our friendship?" he asked softly. "Please?"

Sydney looked at his hand. She remembered the sound in Lauren's voice when she spoke about Jermaine. Even during the very worst days of their relationship, Marcus had always been a supportive friend. She felt her resolve weaken. "I guess . . ." she started.

Marcus released a loud sigh of relief. "Listen, I agree, this isn't the place to talk. This week is absolutely crazed with the achievement awards ceremony that I'm planning at the Youth

Center. May I take you out for coffee on Saturday evening or something?"

"I've already got plans," Sydney hedged, purposely omitting the name of who she was going to be with on Saturday.

"Fine," Marcus replied, refusing to be deterred. "I've got tutoring on Monday, but what about next Tuesday?"

Throwing caution to the wind, Sydney nodded her head and whispered, "You've got a date."

12
LAUREN

Lauren pulled up to the back door of the Better Day Women's Shelter, popped her trunk, and hopped out of the car, her eyes darting every which way. She had to admit that she was getting used to the fact that not every neighborhood in Hotlanta was as spectacularly pristine as Buckhead, but pulling her Saab, Baby, into a grimy back alley in Decatur, only to be greeted by a woman with more attitude than teeth, was just a little too much for her nerves, considering what they, Sydney and Lauren, were up to.

"You gonna have to pull that car up some — I'm spectin' a delivery, and it'll be here directly," hissed the woman, wiping her wet hands on a stained apron tied around her well-worn, tight, cotton floral dress.

"I-I was just about to drop —" Lauren stuttered.

"Out of the goodness of her heart, my sister was just dropping off some of her most prized possessions for the shelter," Sydney interrupted, walking up behind the kitchen lady and rubbing her shoulders. "How you doing, Ms. Jansen?" she asked.

"Oh, hey, baby — I'm mighty fine, mighty fine, indeed," Ms. Jansen said. "Lord, look at this. She was hiding back there behind the trunk, I couldn't see her face. I knew you had a twin sister, but my word, I ain't never seen two people look so much alike. How you doin', sugar? Come on over here, don't be shy."

Buoyed by a "get over here quick" look from Sydney, Lauren walked awkwardly over to the old lady and fell stiffly into her embrace. "Nice to, um, meet you," she said, patting Ms. Jansen on her back and pulling away as quickly and efficiently as she could. "So, um, Syd, can you, uh, help me get the boxes out of the car?" Lauren asked, jutting her chin toward Baby, hoping it was a strong enough hint to her sister that they needed to get moving. Uncle Larry wasn't going to wait.

"Yes, um, excuse me, Ms. Jansen, while I help Lauren unload. We're going to a lunch meeting with our party planner, and Lauren's paying, so I need to hurry up before she changes her mind," Sydney said, pouring on the charm with a wink.

"Oh, go 'head, sugar — don't let me get in the way of a

free meal," Ms. Jansen said. "I best get back inside, too. Gonna have a lot of hungry moms and kids on my hands in about a half hour, and the Meals on Wheels truck should be here in a few minutes."

"Okay, Ms. Jansen, we're just going to bring the boxes in and we'll be out of the way in a sec," Sydney said.

"Okay, then. It sure was good to meet you, Lauren. You got a mighty fine sister," she said.

"Yes, ma'am, it was good to meet you, too," Lauren said, waving.

Both sisters watched Ms. Jansen as she disappeared into the building, then ducked their heads into the trunk for a quick convo.

"So we're all set with Uncle Larry, right?" Sydney asked as she shuffled through one of the several bags Lauren had stuffed with old skirts and jeans she'd long banished to the back corner of her closet, never to see the light of day again.

"Yeah, I confirmed again on the way over here," Lauren said as she fingered a hot ivory silk BCBG cami she'd stuffed in the bag. She remembered it well — wore it to Homecoming last year under a fab wine-colored Betsey Johnson cropped jacket that she paired with a soft purple tutu. With the tutu, she just couldn't part, even though that, too, would never be rocked again. Once she'd been photographed in it — wearing it in public was no longer an option.

"God, this outfit was so cute!" Lauren gushed.

"Lauren! Focus!" Sydney said, snapping her fingers.

"I am — trust," Lauren said. "Nobody is more focused than me right now."

"Well, what did you tell him we wanted to talk about?" quizzed Sydney.

"I told him that I was bringing you over to introduce him to his niece," Lauren said.

"And?"

"And that we wanted to get his take on what's going on, because he's a neutral party and knows enough background to help us figure things out."

"And? What did he say?" Sydney asked, exasperated.

"And he said it was fine, but we needed to be quick about it because he really didn't need anyone to see us in his house. And he wants us to take a cab so neither of our cars are parked outside."

"We can do that," Sydney said as she walked the bags toward the shelter's kitchen door. "As a matter of fact, that's a great idea, because if Keisha's little friend is still following us, he'll see that our cars are still here and think we're doing what we said we were going to do, which was meet Renaldo here for lunch, right?"

"I guess," Lauren said.

"Don't guess — know," Sydney said. "We have exactly two and a half hours before Renaldo arrives. Let's hope this time he's at least sober, so we can wrap up the details for this party. It's really starting to stress me out."

"Yeah, well, this much I know," Lauren said sarcastically. "I don't have any cash — I hope you have some cab money."

Sydney shook her head and walked into the Better Day. *Some things*, she said to herself, *never change*.

"We need to make a quick stop before we get to our final destination," Lauren told the cab driver as she punched in a message on her cell and snapped it shut.

"Wait, what do you mean we have to make a stop?" Sydney asked, frowning at her sister. "I thought you said Uncle Larry was in a rush."

"It'll be quick. We're just going to pull up to the McDonald's right around the corner from Uncle Larry's house and pick up Jermaine."

"Jermaine?" Sydney boomed. "Who said Jermaine was coming with us? Does Uncle Larry know?"

"Me, and no," Lauren said simply.

"Don't you think the two of us should have talked about this?" Sydney demanded. "I mean, Uncle Larry is already freaked out about us coming to his house, and now you want to bring the bogeyman to his place, too? Are you crazy?"

"Oh, calm down, Syd," Lauren said, peering out the window to get a read on how far they were from the spot where

Jermaine had just told her they should meet. "There's no need for the dramatics. I figured it would be best if we had Jermaine there so that he and Uncle Larry could exchange info. The more we have, the better we'll understand what's up, and the closer he can get to finding out what really happened to his brother."

"But —" Sydney began.

"But it's too late to change this, Syd. We're here," she said, pointing to the McDonald's. Jermaine was standing at the door near the drive-thru, a black hoodie with countless dollar signs covering his face. "Right over there, sir. We're going to pick him up and then head on over to Peeples Street."

The driver did what he was told. Jermaine hopped into the car on Sydney's side and slammed the door behind him. "What up?" he said, pulling his hood off his face to get a better look at the girls. It took him a quick second to figure out who was who; Lauren's smile was just the clue he needed.

"Hey, baby," Lauren said, leaning over Sydney to give Jermaine a peck on his cheek. "I sure am glad to see you."

Sydney sat back and didn't say another word until the three of them walked up Uncle Larry's driveway to the side entrance of his house, a surprisingly modern four-bedroom flat that mirrored the neat row of houses in this particular section of the West End. Lauren rang the bell; Uncle Larry appeared in the door almost instantly.

"What's he doing here?" Uncle Larry snapped.

"I asked him to come," Lauren said. "I can explain."

Uncle Larry's eyebrows were furrowed at an impossible angle. He was not happy. "Get on in here before somebody sees the three of y'all at my door," he said, rushing Jermaine, Sydney, and Lauren into a narrow hallway just inside his home. Uncle Larry took a quick sweep of his driveway and the neighbor's yard to make sure no one was watching, and then quickly shut the door.

Uncle Larry pushed past the trio and led them through his kitchen and into the basement, a lush, dark entertainment room replete with a plasma TV, several couches and chairs arranged just so, a full bar, and a pool table. Whoever decorated down there had the touch; it was gorgeous.

"Wow, this is a pretty nice place you have here," Sydney said.

"You say that like you're surprised," Uncle Larry said.

Lauren held her breath.

"I, um, didn't mean anything by that, really," Sydney said uncomfortably. "I'm Sydney," she added, reaching for her uncle's hand.

"Oh, I thought you were Lauren," he said, bypassing Sydney's hand and pulling her into a warm embrace. "Look at you — y'all ain't changed. I couldn't tell the two of you apart when you were little, and I still can't to this day."

"I'm cuter," Lauren laughed, reaching to Uncle Larry to give him a hug. "This is Jermaine."

"I know who he is," Uncle Larry practically growled, pulling away from Lauren. "I didn't agree to him being here."

"I know, Uncle Larry, but if we can just sit and talk and explain . . ." Lauren started.

"Yeah, about that," Uncle Larry said, looking at his watch. "I don't have a lot of time for the chitchat. Go on over there and sit down on the sofa. Honestly, I don't know how I'm going to be able to help you, and I damn for sure ain't gonna be able to help him."

The trio moved themselves to the sofa, Lauren holding Jermaine's hand to help calm him. It was clear that he was nervous; he still had his hoodie on and kept shifting back and forth on the heels of his Tims. "Actually, we didn't come here for help, we came for information," Sydney said.

Uncle Larry eyeballed each of the teenagers sitting before him, and then slowly sat in his recliner. He stared at them some more, his eyes focusing on Jermaine the hardest. And then, finally, he said, "What do you want to know."

"Well," Sydney said, looking at Lauren and Jermaine, "maybe you can start with telling us why we didn't know you existed until a few weeks ago, and what happened between Dice, my mom, and Altimus."

"And what kind of business Altimus has going on here in the West End," Lauren chimed in.

"And who took out my brother," Jermaine huffed, speak ing up for the first time.

"Now, hold on there, son. I don't know nothing about what happened to your brother," Uncle Larry said, turning his full attention to Jermaine. "That's up to the detectives to sort out, and I ain't no detective. I'm a simple man with a simple job down at the UPS, and I make a point of staying out of other people's 'business.' "

"But you helped me that Saturday . . ." Lauren began.

"You're family," he said simply.

"Exactly," Sydney chimed in. "And I really want to know why we didn't know about you — why our mother named my sister after you but didn't tell us you existed. What kind of family hides relatives?"

Uncle Larry sat back in his chair and stared at Sydney. It seemed like an eternity passed before he spoke again. "Look," he finally said. "Altimus, your stepdaddy, is a lot of things. Legit ain't one of them. Everybody in these parts knows that much, and I'm probably not telling you anything you don't already know."

"Actually, Uncle Larry, we probably know way less than you think," Sydney responded.

"Obviously, if you're tooling around the West End, trying to solve murder mysteries and dating boys you know nothing about," Uncle Larry said, tossing a glare at Jermaine for good measure. Jermaine shifted in his seat; Lauren put her hand on his knee protectively. She did wonder, though, what it was she didn't know about Jermaine that had her uncle so jumpy.

"Uncle Larry, let's just, um, stay on subject, okay?" Sydney said gently. "Tell us this: Why did our mother and Dice break up, and how did Altimus and she get together?"

"Hmm," Uncle Larry started. "Let's just say that Dice and your mama didn't see eye to eye on a few things as it related to her business with Altimus."

"So they all knew each other back in the day?" Lauren asked.

"Knew each other? Shoot, Dice and Altimus were running partners — couldn't check for one without finding the other. They grew up together, right here in the West End. Got into a lot of trouble together, too, when they got into the game. And my sister, Keisha? She was running right there with them."

"Our mother?" Lauren said, confused.

"Yeah, baby," Uncle Larry said softly. "Your mama was just as involved in their, um, business dealings as they were. In fact, half the time, I couldn't figure out if she was doing more of the dirty work than the boys were. The three of them were riding high over here in the West End for a good stretch, too — had money flowing like wine at a wedding. Thing is, not everybody wants to stay stuck in the muck, if you know what I'm saying, and your daddy wanted out of the life."

"Which daddy," Lauren asked, leaning in.

"*Your* daddy," Uncle Larry said. "Dice gonna always be your daddy, no matter what Altimus says or does," he added, clearly getting agitated.

"What happened between y'all?" Sydney asked, noticing that a nerve had been struck.

Uncle Larry swallowed really hard and sucked his teeth. "Like I said, your daddy, Dice, wanted out of the game. But your mother, she wasn't ready to give up all her Gucci and gold — didn't want to hang it up just yet. And she told that to Dice, but Dice wouldn't listen to her. See, he knew that the longer he stayed in the game, the more dangerous it would get for his two pretty little babies. And the one thing he wasn't going to have was his family in jeopardy. But your mama, she had other plans — thought she could keep up the life without any hassle. And when they got to disagreeing about it, Keisha had Dice squashed and went from the ex-man to the next man."

"Altimus," Lauren said quietly.

"But it sounds like you're saying our mother was in the life, too," Sydney said.

"What? Keisha *was* the life," Uncle Larry said, getting more agitated. "Look, I shouldn't be sitting here telling you all of this. It won't mean nothing but more trouble for me. And I've spent many years making sure my name ain't nowhere up in the middle of the mess Keisha and Altimus are into over here in the West End. She told me to stay out of their business a long time ago, when I questioned how she could get with her man's best friend. She told me to take care of my family, and if I knew what was good for me, to let her worry about her own. She didn't have to tell me but once. I know what she's capable of. And now you do, too."

"Does that mean she may have had something to do with my brother's murder?" Jermaine asked, moving forward in his seat.

"I told you, youngblood, I don't know nothing about all of that," Uncle Larry practically growled. "What I do know is that anybody walking around here asking questions and giving people the 'finding the real killer' O.J. line is as good as a dead man walking, son. You should really think about that long and hard.

"Now," Uncle Larry said, abruptly rising from his recliner, "I, unlike the rest of my family, have a legitimate job to get to, and I can't be late." He stood over the trio, his arms folded.

"Okay, then, Uncle Larry," Sydney said, rising; Jermaine and Lauren did the same. "Thanks for, um, everything. It's a lot, but we're going to try to process it all and figure out what to do next."

"I'm not so sure there's much you can do, sweet pea," Uncle Larry said, touching Sydney's face. "Lord, y'all got my mama's eyes, you know. I knew you two would grow up to be some knockouts. Dice and Keisha did know how to make some pretty babies."

"Why, thank you, Uncle Larry," Lauren gushed, squaring her shoulders and squeezing Jermaine's hand.

"Just watch your back — and be careful about the company you keep," Uncle Larry continued, giving Jermaine a slow once-over.

"Yo, out of respect for my girl here, I'm not going to get into it with you," Jermaine said. "But you don't know nothing about me, money. My brother is dead, and all I'm trying to do is find out who did it, and why. That was my fam, B. What kind of man would I be if I didn't question?"

"You'd be alive, fam," Uncle Larry said simply. "Alive." And then, turning to Sydney, he said, "Look, I don't need him walking out of my house in the company of you two, so I need youngblood here to go out first. Y'all go through the garage and get in my car. I'll drop you off at the train station south of the West End stop, so nobody sees you leaving."

The trio moved toward the steps.

"And I suggest that you not come back," Uncle Larry added quietly.

13
SYDNEY

"Okay, I am so not mad," Sydney murmured as she slowly made a three-hundred-and-sixty-degree turn in her full-length mirror. As a result of all the stress over the last month and a half, she'd dropped at least eight pounds without so much as one nasty wheat grass shot. Her once solid size four figure was now nearly a two. More important, the new dark gray stretch True Religion jeans she'd picked up at Jeffrey on her way home from volunteering at the Better Day were fitting like a skinny bitch's dream.

At the sound of her cell phone buzzing across her desk, Sydney hurried out of her closet. "Shoot," she said, just missing the call. Pulling up the call history, she read Jason's name. Immediately filled with guilt, Sydney debated calling him back now or after her coffee date. Finally, she put the phone down and headed into the closet to finish getting dressed.

Ten minutes later, Sydney was still undecided about the sequined print L.A.M.B. long-sleeve T-shirt she wore. Contrary to her normally much more conservative clothing picks, she had decided to celebrate her first time getting her hair blown out in over four years by trying something a little different. As she flipped her now pin-straight tresses, she thought it might be a tad too much. *Marcus is already going to have a heart attack when he sees my hair,* she thought as she pulled it over her head exposing a blue-and-white polka dot bra. Sydney reached for a plain white Calvin Klein wrap top with a deep V-neck. Once she added her red-banded Michele watch and the two-carat diamond solitaire necklace that matched her studs perfectly, she felt ready to go. "Not too bad," she said to her reflection as she smoothed down the already straight middle part so that her slightly bumped hair perfectly framed her clear face.

She grabbed her cherry-red Fendi bag and headed out as soon as she heard a familiar light tapping at her semiclosed bedroom door. "Come in," she called out.

"Miss Sydney, Marcus is waiting for you downstairs," Edwina informed her with a small smile.

"Okay, thanks," Sydney replied as she transferred the contents of the caramel-colored Hogan bag she rocked earlier in the day at school. "Um, quick question: Are my black ankle boots with the steel heel still downstairs?

"Yes, miss," Edwina replied. "Would you like me to send Marcus up?"

"Actually, I'll be down in two seconds," Sydney replied as she tossed in her phone and scanned the room for the new pack of Dentyne Ice she had bought earlier.

"Okay, Miss Sydney," Edwina answered as she headed out the door without another word.

"Where is it, where is it?" Sydney mumbled as she got down on her hands and knees to look under the bed. Not finding it, she stood up, completely frustrated. "What the hell," she grumbled as she gave up her fruitless search, grabbed her bag, and headed down the hall.

"Hey, you got any gum?" Sydney asked as she knocked on Lauren's door. For a moment, Sydney wasn't sure her sister was in the room. But then the huge mound under the messy comforter slowly moved and a headscarf poked out. "What?" Lauren croaked as she turned down the volume on her television.

"Gum," Sydney repeated, stepping into the room. "I've got a date —" she started immediately regretting her slip when the entire head popped out immediately.

"A date, huh? You and Jason are acting extra monogamous for two people allegedly on the low, if you ask me," Lauren teased, leaning over the edge of the bed to snatch her favorite Gucci bag off the floor. "So where's my favorite Brookhaven receiver taking you, and more interestingly, how are you explaining to Keisha that you have a date on a Tuesday night?" she inquired as she searched the bottom of the bag.

"Actually, I'm not going out with Jason," Sydney admitted as she quickly averted her eyes to avoid the look that Lauren gave her.

"Whaaat?" Lauren dragged out her question. "Okay, who are you and where is my sister?" she asked incredulously as she momentarily forgot about recovering the pack of gum. "Sydney Duke, are you playing the field?"

"Oh, Lauren, please," she snapped. "Stop being dramatic and pass me the damn gum. I gotta go. I'm late. He's already here."

Lauren finally handed her a pack of Winterfresh. "Alrighty then," she started to turn back over when she suddenly sat up in the bed. "He's here? In the house?" she asked suspiciously. Sniffing the air like a bloodhound, she screeched, "Wait a damn minute, is that patchouli oil I smell?"

"Shh!" Sydney tried to quiet her sister. "Don't be so loud," she admonished, turning to head out the door. "And yes, I am going out with Marcus. We're just going out for a coffee so that we can talk."

"About what?" Lauren asked as Sydney walked out and

down the hall. "I sure hope you know what you're doing," she called out forebodingly.

"I hope so, too," Sydney mumbled.

"I'm sorry I took so long," Sydney started as she reached the bottom of the staircase and paused for effect. "I couldn't find my —" To her great surprise, instead of Marcus being stunned into silence at Sydney's new and improved hair *and* physique, he was nowhere to be seen. "Um, hel-lo," Sydney called out as she looked around, unsure what was going on.

The sound of her mother's high-pitched laugh made Sydney jump. "Oh, Marcus, you are too funny," Mrs. Duke said in the fake falsetto she used when she fancied herself flirting with a younger man. "It's so good to see you around again. We missed you!"

See, now, this is that bullshit, Sydney fumed to herself, gritting her teeth as she headed toward the kitchen. It amazed her how her mother could be so welcoming to the same guy who just finished cheating on her daughter. *I wonder if she'll ever be half as nice to Jason*, she mused bitterly as she reached the door.

"Oh, Mrs. Duke, you know you're like a second mother to me," Marcus responded in his best "all-parents-love-me" voice. "And I can't tell you how much my mom adores Sydney. She's always saying what a great job you and Mr.

Duke have done." For a split second, Sydney was sure she was about to be sick.

"Why, you be sure to tell your mother I said thank you very much," Keisha continued. "As I'm sure she knows, it's hard keeping teenagers in line."

Unable to take it any longer, Sydney walked into the kitchen, cutting Keisha's "poor suffering mother" soliloquy short. "I certainly hope I'm not interrupting," Sydney said with a little more attitude than necessary. Surprised by her sudden entrance, both Marcus and Mrs. Duke jumped back slightly. Sydney smiled smugly at the shocked look on Marcus's face when he saw her freshly pressed hair. "Hey, Marcus," she offered.

"Hey . . . I mean wow, Syd, you look totally different," he stuttered in reply.

"Yeah, I don't know what possessed her to do that mess when she knows how you feel . . ." Keisha started.

Purposely flipping her hair over her shoulder, Sydney cut her eyes at her mom and headed to the door to the garage to retrieve her boots. "We should probably get a move on before it gets too late. It is a weeknight after all," Sydney replied, choosing not to address her mother's smart-ass comment.

"You're absolutely right, Syd," Marcus said, standing up and straightening out the green polo golf shirt he wore over a gray long-sleeve T-shirt.

"Oh, you guys go ahead and take your time," Keisha

announced generously as she grinned all up in Marcus's face. "Don't worry about the curfew tonight. I trust Sydney is in good hands." Sydney's mouth dropped open at her mother's blatant kiss-up behavior.

"Actually, I've got an early-morning debate team meeting tomorrow, so I plan to have Sydney back well before ten. But thanks anyway, Mrs. Duke," Marcus said with his award winning smile.

"Good-bye, Mother," Sydney offered smartly as she started past Keisha toward the front door with her boots in hand.

Just as Sydney attempted to pass by, Mrs. Duke reached out and grabbed her arm. Yanking her down under the guise of giving Sydney a parting kiss on the cheek, Kiesha hissed directly in her ear, "You better check that attitude at the door and pull this shit back together!" Releasing her, Mrs. Duke turned to face Marcus and said brightly, "You be sure to take good care of my baby!"

"Yes, ma'am," Marcus replied. "I always do."

"Are you okay?" Marcus asked gently as they pulled into the parking space outside the small coffee-and-dessert shop. For the duration of the twenty-minute drive, Sydney barely said a word, and it was definitely making him nervous. "You know, I didn't get a chance to say anything at your house, but you look really great. Your hair —"

"My hair what?" Sydney cut him off as she unbuckled her seat belt. "Please don't attempt to give me grief about straightening my hair, Marcus. In case you've forgotten, you and I are no longer together. Hence, how you feel is no longer my priority."

"Whoa, Sydney, relax," Marcus said quickly. "All I was going to say was that your hair looks good, too. I mean, yes, I prefer it curly and natural but . . ." As Marcus reached out to gently finger a few strands by Sydney's face, chills ran up and down her body like electricity. "This is nice. It's new. And it works for you."

"Thanks," she replied shyly, finally relaxing. "I'm sorry, I didn't mean to snap. I guess my nerves are just bad from Keisha's never-ending craziness."

"No problem. And you know you don't have to explain to me how extra your mom can be," he said as he reached out and briefly touched her hand. "Anyways, you ready?" he asked. Sydney nodded her head in response. "Cool," Marcus replied as he hopped out and ran around to the other side of the car to open Sydney's door for her. "After you, madam," he said with an exaggerated bow.

"Thank you kindly sir," Sydney replied playfully with a curtsy of her own before the two headed inside.

"You know you ain't slick, right?" Sydney asked Marcus semisarcastically.

"What? What did I do now?" he asked as the waitress walked away with their order of two caramel Bavarian lattes and a strawberry shortcake cupcake.

"This is exactly where we came on our first date *and* exactly what we ordered, Mr. Green," she replied accusingly with a playful shake of the head.

"Oh, my, is it?" he asked with a look of feigned innocence.

"Whatever, Marcus, you're ridiculous," Sydney replied as her cell phone started to buzz. Grabbing it out of her bag, she saw the text from Jason that read: Figure yur prob studying, hit me when your done. Hugs, J. She quickly put it back in her bag.

"So does Jason know you're here with me tonight?" Marcus asked plainly.

"What?" Sydney asked, once again defensive. "Who said that was Jason?

"Come on, Syd, I can tell from the look on your face," Marcus replied. "Give me a little credit, we were together for over four years."

"I did give you credit; too much, obviously," Sydney retorted as she took a sip from her glass of water.

Sighing deeply, Marcus pulled his locs away from his face. "Okay, okay, this is not what I came here to do with you," he said. Sydney shrugged and looked away. "I asked you here because I miss spending time with you . . . with my friend. I do not want us to fight about what has already happened or what is out of our control." Marcus reached out and grabbed her hand to get her attention. She looked down at the engraved silver ID bracelet on his wrist and slowly up to his face. "I promise not to talk mess about Jason if you'll just drop the whole Dara thing. Okay?"

"Fine," Sydney agreed reluctantly as the server brought their order to the table. She picked up a butter knife and cut the cupcake in half. "Choose," she said, offering first pick.

Marcus smiled gratefully, picked up the smaller half, and took a bite. "Mmm, just as good as the first time," he said.

Sydney smiled at the goofy face he made as she stirred sugar into her coffee. "So things at the Youth Center are crazy, huh?" she asked.

"Yeah, man," he replied. "A lot of changes. But it's all for the good. The kids really enjoyed the awards ceremony. I think we're going to try and do it every year."

"Nice," she replied, blowing the steaming cup before taking a sip.

"So how are things at Better Day? Still having issues finding donations?"

"Actually, things are really improving," Sydney said. "Since I had such success with the Benefit Gala, I'm going to help them plan a huge fundraiser around Christmas. We're really hoping to raise enough funds to move to a bigger facility as well as hire van services for the kids."

"Van services for the kids? For what, to go to the movies?" Marcus inquired.

"That, too, but really so that the kids can go to school in the mornings," Sydney explained. "Our hope is that some of the kids, especially the older ones who are aware enough to stay away from the abusive parent if he shows up, might be able to continue attending their old schools. Instead of having to start over in one of the schools near the shelter because there's no way to get back to their old neighborhood."

"Wow, that's going to be a huge undertaking. I'm really impressed," Marcus praised Sydney.

Slightly embarrassed by the attention, Sydney blushed as she took another sip. "It's not that big of a deal. Like you always say, just doing my part."

"Even still, please keep me posted. I'm sure my mom would love to lend her support," Marcus said, referring to Councilwoman Green's extensive political connections in the community.

"That'd be really great," Sydney murmured, biting into the delicious pink cupcake.

"You know, what ever happened with that little girl, Amira?" Marcus asked as he sipped his coffee. "I remember you were really concerned because she'd been having bad nightmares. . . ."

"Oh, you know, she's doing so much better now," Sydney

enthused. "The nightmares have finally stopped, and she's even playing with the other kids now."

"That's good news for sure."

"Yeah, she's adorable. It's like you can't imagine how horrible it must have been growing up in that environment, with her father beating her mom so badly all the time. Slowly, but surely, she's recovering," Sydney said thoughtfully. "Kids are so resilient. They seem to be able to forgive and move on so much faster than us, huh?"

"Yeah, that's for sure," Marcus said quietly as he drained the last of his cup. The two sat in silence for a moment listening to the soft jazz playing in the background. Marcus finally cleared his throat. "So, um, how you doing with that cupcake?" he asked playfully.

"Just fine, thank you," Sydney responded as she popped the rest of it into her mouth. Her cheeks puffed up like a balloon.

"Mmm-hmm, okay, greedy," he laughed as he glanced at the steel Montblanc watch his mother had given him for Christmas last year. "I certainly hope you don't plan to eat like that at Thanksgiving dinner this year!"

"You know, I do," Sydney laughed. "I'm eating all the turkey, all the candied yams and macaroni-and-cheese that Edwina cooks!"

Marcus laughed loudly. "Remember the first year

we were dating when you came over to my house for Thanksgiving dinner?"

"Oh, yeah," Sydney said slowly. "And instead of slices, you cut the poor turkey into a million little shreds!"

"Whatever, you know my carving skills are on point at all times!"

"Humph, okay, Iron Chef, all I know is I don't want you wielding no kinda knife around me anytime soon," she immediately countered.

Marcus chuckled. "Hey, the only reason my hands were so wobbly was because you were around." Then he thoughtfully added, "I was so busy acting like I could handle it and that I had everything under control. I completely ruined everything, huh?"

Sydney sat quietly. "Yeah, pretty much," she said softly as she stared at the bottom of her now-empty coffee cup. The two shared another awkward moment.

Clearing his throat, Marcus pushed back from the table. "Well, lemme get you home so I can get some rest," he said, dropping a crisp twenty. "You ready?"

"I'm always ready. But the real question is, am I willing," Sydney replied with a suggestive smile.

Marcus shook his head. "Okay now, don't get in trouble, Miss Duke," he said with a chuckle as he stepped back to allow her to exit first.

* * *

Contrary to the silence of the earlier trip, when Marcus pulled his BMW around the Duke's fountain, laughter filled the car. "Oh, my God, you are hilarious," Sydney laughed at his imitation of Principal Trumbull getting excited at the pep rally.

"You know I like to keep you laughing," Marcus replied easily.

"I guess," Sydney said, somewhat sad that their time together had come to an end. "Well, lemme go."

"Okay, no problem," Marcus said, and hopped out to open her door for her.

As soon as Sydney stepped out, Marcus positioned himself directly in front of her face. "You know, sometimes people have to feel the burn to learn to stay away from fire," he whispered softly as he fingered a strand of her hair. Sydney paused and looked down to avoid his piercing stare. "I can't front, Sydney. I definitely miss you. Us. Together. And while I accept that we might not be able to be that way now, in my dreams, you are always the woman by my side when I'm being inaugurated for the mayoral post."

"Marcus, don't," Sydney's voice cracked, betraying all the emotions swirling inside of her as she struggled against her own better judgment.

"I won't," he said. "I'm just saying, I hope you can still see the vision."

Sydney barely closed the front door behind her before her eyes began to sting. Kicking off her boots, she ran directly upstairs, hoping to make it to the safe confines of her room before the inevitable tears began to flow.

"How did it go," Lauren called out from her room as Sydney rushed by.

"Fine, just fine," Sydney tossed over her shoulder as she gently closed her door. Taking extra-deep breaths, Sydney struggled to hold it together. "It's fine, I'm fine," she repeated over and over. As the tightness in her chest and the stinging subsided, her cell phone buzzed again.

Sighing, Sydney grabbed her phone out of her bag before tossing it on her desk chair and heading over to her bed. "I thought he was going to let me call him back," Sydney muttered to herself, assuming it was another message from Jason. To her surprise, it was from Renaldo: Darling. Hit me when you get a chance. Need to review the confirmed guest list to make sure we have everyone before the big night. Smooches. Sydney groaned out loud as Marcus's ominous words, "I hope you can still see the vision," repeated themselves over and over. Of course she could; she just wasn't exactly sure if that included her upcoming holiday party.

14
LAUREN

The bright red bullhorn was as extra as the rotund, orange-colored, sweaty little man yelling into it, but that's what made it all the more fitting. Renaldo, after all, was one to be heard, and on this night, he was going to make sure that the guests at the most spectacular event of the Lake Lanier Thanksgiving season were listening — so that this particular event on this particular evening could go off without a hitch. Which meant that, first and foremost, he needed to keep the guests of the Duke daughters — and the wannabes — in check.

"If your name is not etched in red on this list I have in my hand, it sucks to be you. I will ask you kindly to vacate the premises now to spare yourself any embarrassment," Renaldo shouted into the bullhorn. "For those of you who have a problem understanding the words that are coming out of my mouth, let me make it clear: If you weren't invited, you ain't got to go home, but you got to get the hell up outta here.

"Everyone else who has a gold card featuring Lauren and Sydney's beautiful faces and whose names appear on said guest list will be invited to swipe your card in the Red HOTlanta machine to gain access to the red carpet, which will usher you into the soiree of the year. Please enjoy the musical offerings of DJ Goldfinger as we await the arrival of the fabulous Duke sisters. Thank you."

Renaldo handed the list to one of his many minions, then turned to his personal assistant, whose sole purpose on this evening was to a) keep Renaldo's wineglass full, b) have his Vicodin ready for the popping, and c) clear paths large enough for him to get to and handle whatever fires popped up throughout the evening. There was no room for errors. As it was, he was the only adult at the party, save for the chefs, bartenders, and waitstaff, and Altimus Duke had made it clear that he better have a handle on things. Or else.

And let's just say, Renaldo did not want to even begin to consider what, exactly, "or else" meant. He eyeballed the throng of teens — there had to be at least a hundred and quickly growing, dressed to the nines in the finest gold and red outfits daddy's money could buy — and shook his head, pushed the bullhorn into the assistant's chest, and then started yelling into his walkie-talkie. "Bosco! ETA on the arrival!" he screamed, stomping down the red carpet, his ankle-length gold brocade jacket whooshing hard enough to flicker the candlelight flames that licked the unseasonably warm night air.

"Copy that, Ray — about five minutes over and out," the driver, Bosco, said quietly into his walkie-talkie as he maneuvered the gold stretch Rolls-Royce through the dark, woodsy roads of Lake Lanier. He'd been ordered to take his time getting to the party, even though it was, quite literally, just two minutes away from the resort where the girls had gotten themselves ready and their anxious parents were spending the night. Bosco couldn't see through the partition separating the front seat from the main cabin, but that didn't stop him from glancing through the rearview mirror anyway, wondering just what in the hell the black guy who paid for all of this did for a living to be able to afford to spoil his daughters with such an affair. Shoot, the two-day rental cost for the Rolls-Royce alone was more than $8,000, and he'd heard that dude laid out an additional twenty-five grand to have the car custom-painted — transformed from a shiny, sleek, black machine, into a rich, warm gold tone with red flames painted up the sides, and, after the party, back to black. The suites at Emerald Pointe Hotel, the obviously expensive outfits the girls were wearing, the expansive five-bedroom boathouse, private dock, and exclusive beach he peeped when he took the test run a few hours earlier — it all had to add up to pretty much more than his and his wife's yearly salaries put together. The thought of it made Bosco sick — as did the laughter coming from the back cabin.

"Come on, turn the music up, it's a damn party already," Lauren insisted, shooing Donald toward the control panel that already had T.I. overloading the speakers. Sydney was sitting quietly in the far corner, acting like she had a million things on her mind — and none of them about that fine-ass boy she was sitting beside. In fact, her BFFs/support system/groupies Rhea and Carmen were doing more to entertain the boy than Syd was, which was a crime and a shame, Lauren thought, because had *she* noticed Jason when she was a single, unspoken-for woman? Oh, best believe she'd have been riding shotgun on Mr. Danden's lap. She hoped her sister would pull it together and get focused before they arrived. The party was going to do what it do, and there wasn't anything either of the two of them could change now, no matter how much last-minute worrying, begging, pleading, and barking she did to make sure Renaldo was handling, as she put it, "All the little but important details that'll make or break a party." The way Lauren saw it, Renaldo had his check, he was being paid to do his job — leave it to the professionals to sort out. How-some-ever, Lauren wasn't about to study any of this too long: She looked fly, her party was about to be the straight fire, and Jermaine had just called to say he was on his way. She was good.

"Wait, dammit — you're going to make me spill my drink," Donald laughed easily as he hoisted up his Diet Mountain Dew Code Red.

"Forget turning it up, how about turning it off," Jason said, pushing a CD into Donald's face. "Pop that in, playa."

"Oh, a man who knows how to take charge — work, Sydney, you know how to pick 'em!" Lauren yelled, completely oblivious to the blush that rushed across Sydney's face, which read, quite clearly, "Sit back and calm the hell down — you're embarrassing me."

"No worries, J. She may be acting all shy now, but I guarantee you by the end of the night, it's going to be a totally different story," Lauren predicted, snatching the CD from Jason's hand and shoving it into the player. Sound unheard, she pumped the volume and practically blew out everyone's ears when a brand-new underground Jay-Z mix pumped through the speakers.

"Aw, shucks — let me find out Jason Danden still got that East Coast flava in him!" Lauren said, nodding her head hard to the beat and gyrating on the leather seat.

"Lord, help us through," Sydney sighed, shooting a weary look at Rhea and Carmen, who, too, were rocking out to the music. Rhea, sensing her best friend's nerves were being worked, patted Sydney's hand to help settle her.

Jason chuckled and shot a knowing glance toward

Sydney. "Yeah, um, you know, I'm from New York, so I can't exactly get rid of the, um, East Coast flavor."

Sydney smiled back as she punched SPEED-DIAL for Renaldo, and all at once signaled Lauren to turn down the music. "I just want to make sure everything is all right," Sydney started for what felt like the fiftieth time since they had gotten into the Rolls.

"Syd, just let it go — we're already on our way to our hot party. You should be chillin' and getting ready for your star turn on our red carpet. Time to do the last-minute panty-line check and get focused!"

Sydney turned off her iPhone and sat up. "What, exactly, would someone who doesn't wear panties know about lines?" she teased as she bumped up her roller-set curls and adjusted the thin gold straps of her fringed Ungaro minidress.

"Oh, you know wha —" Lauren started in response.

"Ladies, ladies, ladies! We're here — we've arrived. The red carpet awaits!" Donald said, clapping. "Save the Saturday Night Smackdown for next week. We've got to go to work!"

"Yay!" Lauren said, throwing up a "hoorah" cheerleader hand for good measure and grabbing her 14-K gold compact out of her purse to check her lip gloss and powder. "Um, Rhea, Carmen, darlings, let me by — my sister and I really should be the first ones out of the car. Wouldn't want the paparazzi to get it confused."

Sydney rolled her eyes, shook her head, and willingly moved closer to her girls to avoid Lauren's mad rush to be the first one out of the car. Lauren was giggling like a child on Christmas morning as she waited for the driver to open the door. "Ooh, my fans await!" she said to no one in particular as the doors opened to a crowd of literally one hundred and fifty or so of their closest friends, all screaming at the top of their lungs. Spotlights searched the starlit sky, and one was trained right on the Rolls-Royce. Goldfinger queued the music — "Party Like a Rock Star" blasted through the speakers as Lauren gingerly stepped her perfectly pedicured Vamp Red toes onto the red carpet, smoothed out her red Carmen Marc Valvo, and bounced to the music, mouthing the words and tossing beauty queen waves to the crowd. She stopped and struck a pose for the photographers, putting on the glamour puss she and Donald had perfected back at the hotel. One for YRT, yes, sir.

But Lauren's fabulousness was instantly forgotten (except in her own mind, of course) when Jason stepped out of the Rolls and extended his hand to help Sydney out — so loud were the cheers you would have thought he'd just thrown the winning touchdown. After several individual and couple shots, Sydney and Jason paused next to Lauren to pose for flicks. The photographer's flashes were punctuated by squeals of "Ohmigod — I knew something was up with them!" and "Damn, Sydney done upgraded, fo sho." Sydney continued to smile as she wrapped her arm around Jason's muscular arm and gave it a little squeeze, as a signal for them to move down the candlelit red carpet. Like the perfect escort, Jason accommodated her wishes, and the newly minted couple stepped forward. From all the energy in the air, Sydney was clear this was a big moment . . . how big she had no idea.

Lauren wouldn't allow for such folly, though. "Where's the stage? Where's Renaldo? And where is my drink? Seriously? I need you on point, people — this is my damn night! Somebody needs to come with it! Syd? Get your boy!"

"Oh, gosh, Lauren! Sydney! Welcome. Welcome," Renaldo gushed, rushing up to the girls as if on cue, bullhorn in his right hand, cell phone in the left, assistant with drinks in hand bringing up the rear. "A signature cocktail, ladies?" he said, snapping his fingers to signal the assistant to hand over the drinks — a pretty pomegranate, rosewater, lime squash concoction served up in martini glasses that had been dusted with gold-colored sugar. The sisters graciously accepted their cocktails and let Renaldo lead the way. "The stage is set up in the great room. I've a special signal arranged for Goldfinger to play Ludacris's 'Georgia' the moment you're up and ready and there's a critical mass of friends on the dance floor. Everyone is swiping their red cards to gain entrance as we speak."

"Perfect," Lauren said. "Now, be a dear and see if Jermaine Watson has arrived. He's my special guest, and he's supposed to be here waiting for me. Thank you."

"Uh, um, not a problem, um — you're Lauren, right?" Renaldo asked, his cocktails and prescriptions starting to get the best of him.

"That's correct," Lauren said, a tad disdainfully. She reached into her purse and pulled out her dedicated cell, which she'd set on vibrate earlier, to be sure she didn't miss Jermaine's phone calls. Though she was sure it hadn't rung since the last time her man dialed her digits, she still checked to see if there were any missed calls. Nothing. She slammed the phone shut. "We'll be on the stage," she said, signaling to Donald to follow her.

"Jason and I are going to go greet our guests," Sydney said.

"See you at the top," Lauren said, turning on her heels and grabbing Donald's hand. She was grateful for the breeze that blew through the glass French doors running the length of the back of the house. Renaldo had wisely left them open to keep the air circulating among the hundreds of people who were piling in and working up a sweat in the great room, and to give easy access to those who chose to have drinks and food from the four-course buffet set out on the bonfire-lit beach.

Lauren had barely gotten into her over-the-shoulder sexy dance on the stage when she noticed the commotion — saw a swarm of her guests rushing through the French doors and out onto the beach. "Aw, damn," said Donald. "Can't take your people nowhere. I told you to get security."

"Shut up, D," she laughed nervously. "It's probably that hooker Julia out there dropping it like it's hot. You know how her big booty draws a crowd."

"Indeed," Donald said, craning his head to see if he could catch a glimpse of what — or who — was causing the ruckus. "Regardless, we better get out there."

Donald took Lauren by the hand as they walk/ran to the patio leading out to the beach, where a massive crowd had gathered. It was quiet, save for the music blasting from the system and what sounded like two guys exchanging heated words.

"I'm just saying, you obviously ain't handling your business too well, money, because if you were, your girl, Sydney, here wouldn't have been out on a date with me last week," Lauren heard one of the voices say.

"You guys, just stop — this is so fifth grade, seriously," Sydney pleaded. The desperation in her voice made Lauren push harder through the massive collection of bodies gathered around what turned out to be her sister, Jason, and Marcus.

"Well, you couldn't have been handling business too well yourself, *money*, because it's pretty obvious who she chose," Jason said, folding his arms. "In case you missed it? We came together. This right here?" he added, nodding at Sydney, "All me, playa. All me."

"Man, listen, Sydney Duke and I been *doing* the relationship thing for four years. You were in the limo for five minutes. Seriously? You need to back up and let a grown man handle grown-man business."

"Aw, it's like that, playa?" Jason asked as he took off his suit jacket and his boys — read the entire football team — crowded around him. "Grown man, huh?"

Lauren got to the center of the action just as Jason's fist pounded down on Marcus's left cheek like a hammer on a nail head.

"Oh, my God!" Sydney screamed. "Stop it! Just stop it!"

"Syd, get out of the way!" Lauren yelled, pulling her sister from the fracas, which turned into an all-out brawl, with half the football team bouncing on Marcus and his crew. Fists were flying, girls were screaming, martini glasses crashed against the patio and crunched under fast-moving feet that tried to carry their owners away to a safe perch where blows could be avoided but the drama could still be seen.

"Are you all right?" Lauren yelled over the rumble.

"Get off of me — I have to get out of here," Sydney said, pulling her arm from her sister's grip. She ran toward the backstairs leading up to the bedrooms. "I can't believe this is happening!"

"Donald!" Lauren yelled. "Do something!"

"Hold up, what you want me to do? Them some big boys," Donald huffed.

"Donald!" Lauren yelled.

Just as she tried to rush through the crowd to get to her sister, Lauren's dedicated phone vibrated. Jermaine.

"Go get Renaldo and tell him to grab every grown man in the house!" Lauren hissed to Donald as she snatched open her purse and reached for her phone. As her fingers touched it, the crowd surged against her, knocking her purse and the phone onto the floor. "What the hell!" she yelled, trying to keep the bundle of bodies and feet from trampling her phone.

The party dissolved into total chaos.

The flickering light from the candles that lined the ceiling-high shelves caught Lauren's eye, making her remember that they lined the stage, which was equipped with — yes! — a microphone. She tore away from the tangle and rushed over to it.

"Marcus Green. Get your granola-crunching, backpacking, patchouli-wearing behind off of my sister's guest!" she yelled into the microphone, just as Goldfinger stopped the music. "And all you Neanderthals who've turned my party into the WWE SmackDown, I'm gonna need y'all to get the hell on. Now!"

Lauren's directive had some impact, but it wasn't until Renaldo and several of the waiters and the bartender started pulling boys off of each other that it actually calmed down. When Marcus started yelling, it got really quiet.

"Forget this, man," Marcus said, standing up and wiping blood from the corner of his mouth. "I don't need this."

"You don't want this is what you meant," Jason said, straightening out his shirt and dusting the sand off his suit pants.

"Nah, man, it's all you. But just remember this: You may be playing in the game, but I'm always going to take home the trophy," Marcus said, backing away from the line of football players who were again gathering behind their team co-captain.

"Um, excuse me!" the bullhorn sounded.

Lauren craned her neck to see who in the world was yelling into the electronic megaphone, and, more, just who was calling attention at her party, in her house.

"Just what trophy would you be talking about, Marcus Green?" the girl yelled again in the bullhorn.

This time, Lauren didn't need any introductions; it was Dara. She knew the voice, and it was as clear as crystal. This girl had lost her damn mind showing up at her party. Lauren snatched off her shoes and practically Kung Fu leaped off the wooden structure onto the dance floor, just feet away from her best-friend-turned-nemesis.

"Um, excuse me — There was a weight limit to the guest list and you didn't make the cut. I'm going to need you to vacate the premises," Lauren snarled into the microphone.

"Oh, aren't you just the little Chris RockNot," Dara yelled into the bullhorn. "I was just trying to get some clarity and give some clarity on a few things, honey. And then I'll be leaving."

"I think we're all pretty clear that you're a tramp-ass hooker who can't be trusted around other people's boyfriends," Lauren yelled. "No more clarity necessary."

"Oh, sweetie, trust. There are some things you and your sister most certainly need to know, and I'm here to make sure you hear it from the horse's mouth: I'm having Marcus's baby."

The room erupted into gasps audible enough, Lauren was sure, to be heard over the expanse of Lake Lanier. Jason folded his arms and chuckled; his football buddies knocked him on the arm and back in celebration, like he'd just won a prize. Marcus, on the other hand, looked like he was about to vomit.

Lauren didn't know what to do — barely squeezed out a "What did you just say?"

"Oh, you heard me. I'm having Marcus's baby. So all of this chitchat about trophies and sloppy seconds and that damn Sydney Duke can really just, oh, I don't know, come to a halt," Dara said. And then she really leaned into the bull-horn and said, "Now!"

"Oh, you know what?" Lauren said, rushing Dara, "I will beat your ass like you stole something." But just as her hands got a good grip on Dara, a pair of arms embraced her in a bear hug. "Let me go! Let me go, dammit! Stop it!"

"Baby, it's me — you don't want to hit her, trust me," Jermaine said, holding Lauren in his arms. She instantly calmed. "From what I can see, she's not worth it."

"Oh, what do you know, Boyz N the Hood?" Dara yelped into the megaphone.

"Look, you don't know me, and I don't know you, so there's no reason for us to be getting into it. But you messin' with my girl right now, and she's asked you to leave, so leave."

"Why don't you show her the door and then walk through it with her," an even louder and deeper voice boomed. Lauren turned toward the source, praying a miracle of all miracles, that it wasn't who she thought it was — Altimus.

"Yo, Mr. Duke," Jermaine said, releasing Lauren from his grip and raising his hands like someone had a gun to his chest. "I was invited, you know what I'm saying?"

Altimus continued walking toward Jermaine, the crowd parting like the Red Sea to let him inch closer to his daughter and her boyfriend. "I told you to stay away from my daughter, and I meant it. Looks like somebody's hard of hearing, though," Altimus said easily, eerily.

"I, um, I . . ." Jermaine started.

"No, no, partner — see, it's over now. You and me? We need to go on outside and have a little talk. And then after I'm finished talking . . ."

Jermaine didn't let Altimus finish his sentence. He gave Lauren a look that said, "I'm sorry," and then took off toward the stage. He hopped up onto it, then onto the massive speakers that flanked the left side, and jumped over the heads of a throng of chatty girls who might as well have settled in with some popcorn, so enamored were they by this piece of ghetto Negro theater. Starring the Dukes, of all people — Buckhead's premier African-American family.

Jermaine landed somehow on his feet and disappeared through the door and out into the November night.

YoungRichandTriflin would win a Pulitzer once it finished sorting through all this mess.

15
SYDNEY

As they turned up the long, windy driveway to the Duke estate, the silence in the backseat of Altimus's car was deafening. In fact, the only thing Sydney could hear above the beat of her heart was Lauren's murmured prayer.

"Oh, God, please don't let her kill us. And if she should kill us tonight, O Lord? Dear God, please let it be swift and painless. Amen," she finished with a sign of the cross.

"Hey. We're coming up the driveway now," Altimus said gruffly into his Bluetooth. "They'll meet you in my office. Bye." He clicked off the call and looked up at the rearview mirror. As his eyes met Sydney's gaze, they momentarily narrowed to slits. Positive she had just been issued the kiss of death, Sydney gulped.

"Sydney, I'm really scared," a pale-faced Lauren whispered.

"Me, too, sis, me, too," Sydney admitted as she reached for Lauren's hand. The car finally came to a stop in front of the front door.

"Your mother is waiting for the both of you inside my office," Altimus said to the girls despite continuing to look straight ahead. "Go 'head."

As soon as the girls stepped out and closed the car door behind them, Altimus pulled away without another word. They both looked at the car as it disappeared back down the driveway. "Do you think we should make a run for it?" Lauren asked with a slight tremor in her voice.

"And go where?" Sydney asked. "There's nowhere that we can hide, no one who can protect us from him except Mom. We just have to make her believe us."

Lauren nodded her head silently. "She might be crazy, but she's our mother. At the end of the day, blood is thicker than water. She's not going to take the word of some man over her own flesh and blood, right, Syd?"

"I hope so, Lauren, I really hope so," Sydney replied grimly as she walked toward the house.

"Close the door, sit your asses down, and don't, I repeat do not, open your mouths," Keisha hissed as soon as Sydney and Lauren stepped half a foot inside Altimus's office. Seated in his oversized leather chair behind the enormous mahogany desk, Keisha looked like the female version of Don Corleone from *The Godfather* to the two terrified girls.

"So I take it the two of you think that your stepfather and I are a couple of fools, huh?" she said in a very low, very lethal tone of voice. The twins simultaneously shook their heads viciously. "But you must," she goaded. "You must think we're stupid. Because otherwise, why would you behave the way you do?" The girls shifted uncomfortably on the plush burgundy loveseat. "Why," she paused for emphasis, "why would you disrespect us like this?

"I mean, just so I'm clear. Your stepfather and I allow the two of you to throw a no-holds-barred holiday party for damn near everyone in your entire school at our million-dollar lake house, and instead of behaving like mature young women with a lick of home training, you end up in the middle of a melee? Thousands of dollars wasted, a fistfight in my living room, and someone that I wouldn't even want to share the same sidewalk with, standing up in the middle of my damn house, so called representing my child? This is how you repay us?"

Lauren gulped audibly.

"Are you satisfied with yourselves? In a matter of months, the both of you have managed to make our family the laughing stock of the entire community. Oh, but I guess that shouldn't matter because Altimus and I, we're nothing but a couple of dummies. So who cares what people say, right? Who cares how hard we've worked to secure a better life for the two of you ungrateful little heiffas; this is the *Lauren and Sydney Show*. And I guess we're just lucky to be here." Sydney could feel the perspiration forming on her upper lip.

Keisha stood up and walked over to stand directly in Lauren's face. "Look at you, sitting here with that fifty-dollar manicure, five hundred-dollar weave, and three-thousand-dollar outfit that *I* bought your silly behind; running around pretending to date a pansy so that you can screw a future convict. You think you're thugged out, Little Ms. Dance Squad? Huh? Is that what it is? Clearly you do. 'Cause instead of being grateful for the privileges, instead of trying to take advantage of what's around you, you're up in the middle of the hood trying your damndest to either get knocked up or knocked out. And the worst part is, I can't tell which!" Lauren cringed after every word as if she'd been physically slapped.

Then Mrs. Duke walked over to stand in front of Sydney. However, instead of screaming at her, she just started to laugh. Not knowing what to make of her mother's behavior, Sydney unsuccessfully tried to sneak a look at her sister without turning her head. "You kill me, Sydney," Mrs. Duke finally said when she stopped laughing. "Do you hear me, you KILL me with your low-budget Nancy Drew act. Running around trying to find clues, and you don't even understand the case. You're pathetic," she hissed. "So hell-bent on this whole save my daddy campaign and you don't even KNOW your father!" Hot tears formed in Sydney's eyes as she struggled to remain silent. "Since you want to know so badly, let me tell you again. Your father is a piece of crap. Period. Nothing more and nothing less than a worthless excuse for a man who, when push came to shove, wasn't willing to do what it took to handle his business. So now that you know, you can stop trying to be Captain-Save-A-Convict and focus on getting Marcus back. Because you might play the role of Lil' Miss Bleeding Heart, but at the end of the day, your tastes are real high maintenance. And being the captain of some damn high school football team certainly ain't no NFL guarantee!" Unable to hold them back, Sydney sat stone-faced as the tears finally fell.

Keisha stepped back and turned her back on both of the girls. "I'm just tired of y'all," she sighed. "As long as you've been alive, I've always done everything I can to make sure you were well taken care of. I swore my children were going to have everything they could ever dream of . . . regardless of what it might cost. And this is how you repay me. I give you the world and you give me your ass to kiss. Humph, well I'm done. The both of you are some ungrateful brats. And I'm really starting to wonder if maybe Altimus and I should just send you both away until you learn to appreciate what you have here. I'd be very curious to see what your beloved father or even your ghetto Romeo can do for y'all when you're cleaning up shit in a barn on a farm in Africa!"

Unable to sit still a moment longer, Lauren blurted out, "Mom, you don't understand what's really going on. I swear to you, we weren't trying to be disrespectful! It's bigger than the party! You're in danger! We're all in danger!"

"What the hell are you talking about," Keisha said, spinning around. Her eyes were nothing but narrow slits as she stared at Lauren like she wanted nothing more than to smack the taste out of her mouth.

"Tell her, Sydney," Lauren pleaded. "Tell her what we found out."

"It's true, Mom," Sydney sniffled as she wiped the tears away. "I wasn't trying to be ungrateful. I just, I didn't understand why I couldn't ever see Dad. But that's nothing, 'cause we found out that Altimus —"

"Altimus what?" Keisha snapped. "Please tell me what you found out about my husband. I surely want to hear this mess. What did you find out? Please tell."

"Mom, I know this is going to sound crazy, but Altimus is not the person he pretends to be," Sydney continued carefully, trying to gauge her mother's reaction as she went along. "He's living a double life. Trust us, he does much more than just run the car dealerships."

"Oh, really, " Keisha said in feigned disbelief. "And what else is he doing?"

"Mom, he's a killer!" Lauren blurted out. "A straight-up gangster. You didn't see him when he got really angry . . . I mean, *everybody* in the West End is convinced that he killed Rodney Watson, and I, I mean, we think they may be right!"

"It's bigger than that, Mom," Sydney continued quickly on the heels of her sister's outburst. "I think he may have even had something to do with setting Dad up to go to jail. Which means that Dad is innocent! He didn't just abandon us!"

"Mom, this is for real. And he knows that we know something." Lauren continued working herself into a full frenzy as she looked over her shoulder at the door and back to Mrs. Duke. "We need to get out of here. Not now, but right now! We are not safe!"

Mrs. Duke's facial expression went from sarcastic disbelief to dead seriousness. "So it's not just the two of you who think that Altimus is leading a double life?" she asked thoughtfully.

"Absolutely not," Sydney insisted. "Dad has hinted, Aunt Lorraine . . ."

"Shoot, anyone who figured out that I was Altimus's daughter always acted like they were about to get it," Lauren continued cryptically. "It's crazy. Not for nothing, the one time I met Rodney he said something about Altimus having to ante up or something like that! Whatever he said, Mom, for real, this is not good!"

Keisha inhaled deeply, frowned, and shook her head. "No, you're right, this isn't good." She replied so calmly that Sydney thought she must be in shock.

"Er, um, okay, but don't you think we should be making moves to pack our stuff and go to the cops?" Lauren asked. "He could be back at any moment . . ."

"Oh, I'm sure he will be," Keisha answered with a sigh as she walked over to the desk and sat on the edge facing the girls. "Which is why I need to hurry up and say what I have to say. Because, as I'm sure Lauren can attest, Altimus is not the one when he's pissed. And quite honestly, it's high time you two got with the program and started acting like you had some damn common sense before every last one of us goes to jail!"

"Excuse you?" Sydney responded without thinking.

"No, excuse *you*," Mrs. Duke snapped. "Where the hell do you think all the money to keep your little spoiled behinds on weekly shopping sprees comes from? Ain't that many damn leased luxury cars in the world!" Lauren's mouth dropped open. "Oh, save the theatrics, Lauren. You stay watching BET. You know exactly what time it is. Now listen very carefully to what I'm about to say.

"Altimus had nothing to do with setting your father up. At all. But yes, the two of them were business partners back in the day. And they were both deep in the streets. Between Altimus and your father, the entire West End was on lock. There wasn't an illegal dollar being made that they weren't getting a percentage of in their heyday."

"You- you- you knew Dad was into something illegal and you were okay with that?" Sydney stuttered.

"Um, and how the hell else were we going to pay the rent every month, smart-ass?" Keisha retorted angrily. "Last time I checked, landlords didn't accept food stamps." Humbled, Sydney looked down at the floor. "And like I said, we were doing good. But when I got pregnant, your father started losing focus. He just kept stressing how he didn't want to miss out on raising his babies." Keisha laughed evilly. "A lot of good all that trying to get out of the game did him, huh?"

"You sound like you're glad that he went to jail," Lauren said incredulously. "I thought you loved him."

"Love don't have shit to do with survival. When your weak-ass father stopped taking care of his business, I had to step up and handle mine. So I made a choice. I chose to be with the man who could and would do whatever it took to make sure that me and mine were cared for. Period. Altimus goes hard for me and I will ride for him. It is what it is."

"So our stepfather is a drug dealer, is that what you're telling us?" Sydney asked Mrs. Duke contemptuously.

"Altimus is a lot of things — not all of them legal — but what you need to know is, he's a good man who understands what loyalty means. In turn, he expects and deserves that from the both of you," retorted Keisha, ignoring Sydney's comment.

"But- but- but-" Lauren stammered.

"But nothing," Keisha answered.

"But drugs, Mom? As anti-drugs as you are?" Sydney questioned.

"Sydney, I said he was into a lot of things. You said drugs," Keisha corrected swiftly. "Your stepfather is a businessman. He provides transportation. Packages come through Georgia and need safe transport to various destinations. What these packages are is irrelevant. What matters is that the owners are willing to pay a lot of damn cash to make sure that *one*, their items get where they're going, and *two*, that no one knows about the deliveries. *That* is the real Duke family business."

"So then why does everyone think he has something to do with Rodney getting killed?" Lauren asked.

"In this line of business, sometimes there are unexpected incidentals," Keisha shrugged nonchalantly. "Charge it to the game. Nothing personal I assure you." Lauren and Sydney looked at each other as her words sunk in.

"As I'm sure you can now understand, the last thing this *family* can afford is to have the two of you drawing unnecessary attention to Altimus. Your snooping and running amuck is becoming a liability. And that makes us all vulnerable. So

I suggest you both get with the damn program. Because whether you like it or not, you're part of this family. If one falls, we *all* go down. Do you understand what I'm saying to you?"

"Yes, ma'am," Sydney and Lauren mumbled, too afraid to say anything else.

"Good. Now, go up to your rooms and stay there till I figure out an acceptable punishment for the stunt you pulled at my damn lake house!" The girls stood up wordlessly and turned to leave. "Oh, and Sydney," Keisha called out as the girls headed through the door. "The next time you talk to your father or his trifling-ass sister, Lorraine, I suggest you keep the conversation to what's happening at school. I'd hate for him to miss out on the rest of his daughters' lives trying to prove a point. Am I clear?"

"Crystal," Sydney replied.

As soon as she reached her bedroom, Sydney's knees gave out on her and she fell to the floor. Sobbing hysterically, she couldn't believe what had just happened. Her stepfather was a murderer and her very own mother was A-OK with this. Curled up in the fetal position, Sydney couldn't imagine what to do to next. There really was nowhere to go that the twins would be safe and, what's worse, as Keisha implied, now that they knew the truth, both she and Lauren might be considered accomplices. Sydney gave up trying to make sense of how her entire existence had unraveled in a matter of moments and just bawled.

When she could finally cry no more, Sydney picked herself up gently and headed into the bathroom to wash her face. Her red eyes were almost swollen shut and saliva had dried on the side of her cheek. "Yuck," she said, reaching for her Lotus Moon facial cleanser. As she squirted a dime-sized drop of the organic cleanser in the palm of her hand she thought about how expensive the thirty-five-dollar bottle was compared to stuff sold in most drugstores. Feeling extremely guilty, Sydney immediately washed it off of her hand and rinsed her face with plain water instead. When she finished, Sydney headed back into her bedroom and started to take off her clothes. Stripping down to her tank top and pink striped Cosabella boyshorts, she climbed into her bed and lay under the covers watching the ceiling fan spin.

"Hey, Syd," Lauren softly whispered at the door before she pushed it open and entered sporting a similar red-eyed, puffy-face look. Sydney slowly turned her head to watch her sister walk over to her bedside. "I don't want to be alone," Lauren said as once again the tears began to fall. Sydney moved over and pulled the covers back to allow her sister to join her in the bed. Silently, the two girls clung to each other as if their lives depended on it.

16
LAUREN

It felt like a knife — hot and searing, running back and forth across her abdomen, digging deeper and deeper still. It woke Lauren clean out of her sleep — a pain so abrupt, so powerful, she sat straight up in Sydney's bed, momentarily unaware of just where, exactly, she was. She clutched her stomach and doubled over — tasted the bile that crept up into her throat. She was going to throw up, for sure.

"What's wrong?" Sydney asked, sitting up. She rubbed Lauren's back.

"As if there isn't enough going on, now after all that damn faking I really do have my damn period," Lauren seethed. "This is so not happening."

"Be glad for the little things," Sydney said. "You could be walking around with a baby bump and a megaphone."

"Good God, what the hell was that?" Lauren said, rubbing her stomach and fighting back her urge to hurl.

"That was four years of wasted energy," Sydney said, rubbing her temples. "I hope she and Marcus are happy. And if it doesn't work out," Sydney added, whispering and looking around her room conspiratorially, "maybe he and Keisha could get it on, seeing as she loves him so damn much."

Lauren chuckled. "See, you need to stop — she might hear you," she said. "And I might throw up."

"Eww — not in my bed. I'm afraid I'm going to have to ask you to leave now," Sydney said, gently pushing her twin out of the bed they'd shared all day long.

"Whatever," Lauren said. "I'm going to the bathroom to handle my business and swallow a half a bottle of Aleve, and then I'm going to crawl downstairs to get Edwina to fix me a cup of raspberry tea. Maybe that'll settle my stomach — at least from the cramps, anyway. You want anything?"

"Just for this day to be over," Sydney sighed. "And for things to get back to the way they used to be."

"I'm with you there," Lauren said. "Don't hold your breath, though."

It was Sunday night, which meant that Edwina had the night off and was most likely with her family, which also meant that Lauren would have to fend for herself in the kitchen. That was bull. Because Lauren couldn't even begin to fathom where Edwina would stash the raspberry tea, though she figured she could venture a guess if she thought about it hard enough. But now that they were here, the cramps were coming fast and hard, and really, Lauren just didn't want to be bothered with the microwave and the sugar and the teabag, let alone walking back up the stairs. She snatched open a cupboard or two — saw canned vegetables, pasta and taco boxes, seasonings, cereal. "Where in the hell?" she muttered under her breath. And then, just as quickly, she found the teabags.

Box in hand, she headed for the cupboard and pulled out one of the heavy Salty Dog mugs her mother collected on their last trip to their condo in Hilton Head, South Carolina.

And then she heard them.

"Yeah, well, I know this much. They better have gotten into their thick little heads that this ain't a game," Keisha groused from the study, which was just off the kitchen, next to Altimus's office.

"They making things hot, fo sho," Altimus grumbled. "I hope they really heard you, but I didn't know the extent of how much they'd figured out. Ain't but one way that happened; somebody's been snitching. You know we can't afford snitches, Keish."

Lauren's knees began to wobble, but somehow, she

found the strength to tiptoe a little closer to the side of the kitchen closest to the study.

"So I take it you didn't find him?" Keisha continued.

"But I'm on it," Altimus replied. "He won't be able to hide for much longer. I got a friend at Telecom, gonna be telling me everyone he's talking to. It won't be long, trust. I'll get his ass, find out just how much he knows."

They were talking about Jermaine — Lauren knew it. She felt light-headed and wobbly as the combination of the overheard conversation and killer cramps started to get the best of her. She grabbed at her stomach, forgetting she had the coffee mug in her hand. Until, that is, it came crashing down on marble floor.

The footsteps came rushing around her, first Keisha's, then Altimus's.

"What the hell are you doing in here — spying?" Keisha snarled.

"I . . . I . . . was, um . . ."

"You was what?" Altimus demanded.

"I was just getting a cup of tea," Lauren insisted, her eyes swelling with fresh tears as she finished throwing the last pieces of the mug in the trash. "Edwina is off and I have cramps. I just took some Aleve but it wasn't working and so I just came down to fix myself some tea but I couldn't find the teabags and the mug just slipped — it just . . . slipped out of my hand, and I didn't know you two were down here . . ."

Keisha looked Lauren up and down and laughed. "Damn, girl, seems like you get your period every other week. Running around here trying to be Inspector Gadget and can't even fix a cup of tea right," she said. "Look at you." Then, turning to Altimus she said, "Look at her."

Altimus didn't say anything — just glared.

"I'm, um, I'm going to go on back up to my room now," Lauren said. "I don't, um, really want any tea." She had to will her legs to carry her out of the room slowly, even though every part of her being wanted to race back into her bed, under her covers, in the darkness, where it seemed that nothing — and nobody — could touch her.

"What the hell was all that?" Sydney whispered as soon as her sister got to the top of the stairs. Lauren put her finger to her mouth and pointed her sister to her room. The two speed-walked into the room and quietly closed the door behind them.

"No light — no words," Lauren implored, tucking her hair behind her ear so she could hear whether Keisha and Altimus were making their way upstairs. She heard nothing. And then, all of a sudden, there was a buzzing sound, made more pronounced, no doubt, by the fact that her room was absolutely silent.

"What the hell is that?" Sydney said, jumping.

"That's my phone," Lauren said, diving onto her bed. She reached into a tiny hole inside her massive Brookhaven teddy bear and fished out the KRZR. "My boo" flashed across the screen. "It's Jermaine."

"You gonna answer it?" Sydney inquired.

"Look, I just heard Altimus tell Mom that he tapped Jermaine's phone. If I answer that, they're going to trace it straight back to me, and then they'll find him for sure. I can't let that happen, Syd. I just can't."

Lauren held the vibrating phone next to her heart until it stopped moving; tears dripped onto her hand, between her fingers, and onto the phone.

"Don't cry, Lauren," Sydney said, fighting back her own tears. "Please, don't cry."

"Jermaine is in serious trouble," Lauren said quietly. "And it's all because of me."

"It's not you — don't put this on yourself," Sydney said, hugging her sister. "This isn't us. It's our stepfather. I don't know how we're going to make it right, but I do know we can't do this alone."

"Well, unless you got a direct line to The Man himself, it doesn't seem like there's anybody who can help us without getting hurt themselves. Dad's in prison. Jermaine is on the run. Keisha is on Altimus's side. We can't trust anybody," Lauren cried.

"Wait, shhh," Sydney whispered. "I think I hear something."

The two of them were as still as statues — didn't even take a breath or blink their eyes. There was nothing but silence.

Sure their parents weren't listening in, Sydney said, "Why don't we call Uncle Larry."

"No, no — ain't no way," Lauren said almost as quickly as Sydney finished throwing out her suggestion.

"Look, I've been up here going through it in my mind, and the only person that Keisha doesn't know we reached out to — the only person she didn't mention earlier today — was Uncle Larry. She doesn't know about him."

"And you want to take the chance that she finds out?" Lauren said incredulously.

"L, he's the only one who knows all the players," Sydney said. "He knows Jermaine, right?"

"And he practically kicked him out of his house when we showed up with him last weekend," Lauren said. "Didn't seem like Uncle Larry was interested in helping him out. Why would he change his mind now?"

"He may, or he may not. But at least he can help *us* out, give us some advice on what to do."

"I don't know, Syd," Lauren said. "If they have a trace on Jermaine's phone, they could have one on this phone, too.

I'm not one hundred percent sure, but Jermaine is probably the one paying the bill."

"Look, we don't even have to call him. We can have someone else we trust do it," Sydney said.

"Like who?" Lauren asked. "No offense, but Carmen and Rhea? Not. And all of Brookhaven Prep was on hand to see the Duke family saga unfold before their very eyes at the lake house, and everyone is just waiting for more juice to pour into the gossip cup. Ain't no way . . ."

"Donald," Sydney said simply.

"Donald?" Lauren asked.

"Donald. He's clever, discreet — at least when it comes to your business, right? He could call Uncle Larry. Keisha and Altimus would never know," Sydney said. "We can tell him what to ask, and Donald could call, and he can tell us what Uncle Larry said. It's that simple."

Lauren thought long and hard about it. "Seriously, you don't think they'll find out?"

"How could they?"

"I don't know, Syd," Lauren said. "I don't know."

"Look, what's Donald's number, dammit," Sydney asked, pulling her own old-school flip phone from her bathrobe pocket.

"Where'd you get that?" Lauren asked.

"Let's just say I learned a few good lessons from my

little sister," Sydney laughed. "I got this a few days after I saw the phone Jermaine gave to you."

"Alrighty then," Lauren said, taking the phone from her sister's hands and punching in Donald's number. "Let's give it a shot."

Donald answered on the first ring. "Who?"

"D, it's me, Lauren," Lauren whispered into the phone.

"Wow, I didn't realize they had phone service underground," he said.

"What the hell are you talking about, Donald?" Lauren asked.

"I figured that by now, Keish and Al had you and Sydney buried in the backyard under the magnolias and crepe myrtles," Donald said. "You must have stellar service. Who's number is this, anyway?"

"Donald, shut up and listen, okay? I don't have a lot of time."

"Tell me about it," Donald said. "The way Altimus was looking at the lake house . . ."

"D!" Lauren whispered a little louder. "Shut up and listen!"

"Okay, okay, geez," Donald said. "Go."

"I need you to do me a favor," Lauren began.

"Anything," Donald said simply.

"I need you to call my Uncle Larry and get a read on what Sydney and I need to do to help Jermaine," she said.

"Help Jermaine? Don't you think you better focus on yourself? After that damn disappearing act, seems like Jermaine can handle his. You, I'm not so sure about. . . ."

"Donald, please —" Lauren began.

Sydney snatched the phone away from her. "Donald? This is Sydney. Look, I need you to put on your listening ears, okay? No talking. We're in the middle of some really shady stuff that I can't get into right now, but one consequence of it all is that Lauren's boyfriend could get hurt. We need you to call our uncle, who is about the only sane grown-up on the planet who we actually know, and get him to give us some advice on how to protect Jermaine. Do you think you can handle this mission?"

"Come on, baby, do a bear pee in the woods?" Donald asked. "Who's Uncle Larry?"

"Keisha's brother," Sydney answered easily.

"Keish got a damn brother?" Donald yelled. "Good God, what the hell?"

Sydney pulled the phone away from her ear and rolled her eyes. Then she put the receiver back to her mouth. "Donald. Focus," she said tensely.

"My bad," he said.

"We need you to tell him that Altimus and Keisha ran into Jermaine at our party, and that they're looking for him. And then we need you to ask him what we should do to help him get out of this mess, and if he can help."

"Trouble. Looking. Help. Got it," Donald said.

"Are you sure?" Sydney questioned.

"I'm sure," Donald said. "When do you want me to call?"

"Right now," Sydney said, eyeing the clock. It was 10:40 P.M. She gave Donald the number and wished him good luck. "Call me back at this number when you're done, okay?"

"Bet," Donald said, and hung up.

Sydney pushed END on her KRZR and sat silent. Her eyes had adjusted to the darkness by now, so much so that she could make out her sister's sad eyes in the moonlight, shining through the massive half-circle window floating at the very top of Lauren's twelve-foot wall. The architect who designed the room must have been a stargazer, for sure, because he positioned the windows in both the room and the bathroom to create the perfect frame for the moon in the evening and the North Star in the early morning. Lauren would often be much too groggy in the mornings to appreciate its positioning, but on occasion, when the star hung low enough and the sky was dark enough and the clouds were quiet enough, that star practically spoke to her — its shape so clear it almost looked like someone had come along and painted it with glitter against the midnight blue background. Tonight, the full moon was just as clear, providing the glow the two sisters needed to get them through the darkness.

Not even a minute and a half passed before Sydney's vibrating phone rattled them out of their moon-induced haze. It was Donald. Sydney flipped the phone open, pushed the green button, and said a tentative, "Hello?"

"Your uncle said about the only thing you can do for Jermaine," he whispered, "is pray."

17
SYDNEY

"Lauren," Sydney whispered for the third time as she gently shook the mound in the middle of her sister's queen-size bed. "Lauren, wake up!"

"Huh, what's wrong, Syd?" Lauren asked groggily as she finally poked her head out from under the comforter. Clearly disoriented, she propped herself up to turn and look at the black iHome clock on her nightstand through half-closed eyes. Turning back to Sydney, she continued hoarsely, "It's five-thirty in the morning. What are you doing up already?"

"Lauren, listen to me," Sydney continued urgently. "I need you to cover for me." Mid-sentence, Lauren suddenly plopped back down on her bed with securely closed eyes as if she'd just been shot. "Lauren, this is serious," Sydney hissed as she started to shake her sister again. Now it was

Sydney's turn to look at the clock. With every passing minute her window of opportunity was closing and she knew it.

"Relax, I hear you — you want me to cover for you," she mumbled even as she started burrowing back under the covers. "Cover you for what? Where are you going, to meet Jason or something?"

"I'm going to see Dad."

At that, Lauren sat straight up in the bed with her eyes wide-open. "You're going to jail?" she exclaimed.

"Shush! Lower your voice," Sydney quickly admonished her twin as she covered Lauren's mouth with her hand. "You know Altimus is a light sleeper. I'm already cutting this close. He'll be up in a couple of hours for his morning run, so nine out of ten, he's not even in deep sleep anymore."

Lauren tugged Sydney's hand off her mouth. "Um, and how are you planning to make it to the jail, Harriet Tubman?" she immediately questioned. "Last time I checked, Dad is locked up at least an hour or two away and, hello, our car privileges are suspended indefinitely. Not that I could really explain a missing vehicle and what not." She paused to look at Sydney's fitted all-black outfit and was immediately reminded of the lead character from *Alias*, who was a secret agent. "Hmm, good outfit."

"I'm not driving," Sydney whispered back, ignoring the fashion critique. She threw a nervous glance over her shoulder before detailing her plan. "Last weekend when I was volunteering at the shelter, I asked one of the women how she used to go see her boyfriend in jail since he never allowed her to get a driver's license. She told me about this van that drives women and kids up to the correctional facility for about twenty dollars round-trip. Every Tuesday and Thursday, it picks them up at six-fifteen in the morning in front of the City Court and then drops them back off at three-thirty in the afternoon."

"Okay . . ." Lauren started as she wiped the sleep out of her eyes. "But that's still all the way downtown. How are you getting there from here?"

"Well, that's where you come in," Sydney responded. "I've already called for a cab to pick me up down the block in front of the Whittinham's house. When I get back, I'll just have the cab drop me off at school. That way, Keisha will see me riding home in the car service with you."

"Okay, so basically you need me to keep Keisha from being suspicious of not seeing you this morning?"

"Pretty much," Sydney replied, grateful it was making as much sense to Lauren as it did to her when she concocted the plan in the wee hours of the morning. "All you have to do is tell her that you think I mentioned Carmen picking me up early this morning for an English project we're working on. You know, just be vague and then change the subject or something. But to avoid Altimus being suspicious about the alarm being off before he leaves for his morning run, I thought you could come down and reset the alarm after I leave."

"I don't know, Syd," Lauren hesitated. "I'm not saying it won't all work, but do you really think it's a good idea to try to sneak all the way up to the jail?" Lauren questioned with obvious apprehension that was becoming common in her once-confident devil-may-care voice. "What if Keisha still has that 'friend' of hers spying on us at school? She'll totally find out that you were —"

"Listen," Sydney cut her off sharply. "I don't care. I cannot deal with Brookhaven right now. I mean, did you not see Dara wearing that tacky 'Surprise Inside' T-shirt yesterday? Who does that?"

"Yeah, that was kinda messed up," Lauren agreed sheepishly. She vividly recalled the gloating look on Dara's face as her former best friend walked down the hall in the too-tight pink T-shirt, rubbing her stomach as if she was due any minute.

"Okay, then," Sydney said. "And I'm not even going to tell you how angry Jason is with me. Every time I try to explain what happened, he just rolls his eyes and walks away. Shoot, truth be told, it felt like the entire football team was giving me dirty looks."

"Yuck, forget those wannabe thugs," Lauren immediately defended her sister.

"I mean, it's just too much," Sydney sighed. "And we both know there's no way Keisha is about to let me stay home from school. So instead of wasting the day at the mall or something, I'm going see Dad. I just, I really miss . . ." Sydney's voice cracked.

Lauren swung her legs over the side of the bed and put her hand on her sister's shoulder. "Don't get upset, Sydney. I get it. I got you. Just make sure you make it back to school on time for the pick-up. I'll tell the driver to pick us up at four-thirty instead of four o'clock. That should give you plenty of time."

"Thanks, Lauren." Sydney sniffled one last time as she stood up and offered her hand to Lauren. "You ready?"

Lauren accepted her sister's hand and stood up to join her. "Let's make it happen."

"Keep the change," Sydney offered over her shoulder as she hopped out of the red taxicab. Clutching her bronze-colored Gucci bag tightly under her arm, she hurried across the empty downtown street toward the line of women and children waiting to board a nondescript maroon-colored van with the words B. BROWN'S TRANSPORTATION SERVICE written across the side.

"Fold up your strollers before you get up here, and please watch your step, ladies," a weary-looking older black man instructed as he collected the twenty-dollar fee and handed each of the women a ticket before helping them board the van. Sydney cringed as an extremely pregnant girl, who looked no older than fifteen, struggled to squeeze her wide frame down the narrow aisle inside.

"Um, excuse me. Is this the van to the Central State Prison," Sydney asked a frustrated-looking brown-skinned woman holding a crying baby boy on her hip and the hand of a sleepy-looking five-year-old girl with a head full of brightly colored barrettes.

The woman released the little girl's hand momentarily to pop a pacifier in the baby's mouth and turned to Sydney. Giving her simple but clearly expensive outfit a thorough once-over, the woman sneered, "No, it's the line to the pot of gold at the end of the rainbow," before snatching the little girl's hand and stepping forward.

Sydney instinctively reared back. *Damn, did it call for all that*? she questioned mentally as she made a face at the girl.

"Just ignore her. She just mad 'cause she been made this trip too many damn times already," whispered a cute Mexican-looking girl with long black hair. "You're in the right place. This is the van."

Sydney smiled gratefully at the girl. "Thanks, I thought I might've missed it."

"Naw, we're always running about five to ten minutes late 'cause of loading all the strollers and stuff," she responded between snaps of her gum. She, too, looked at Sydney's all-black ensemble up and down. "This your first time, huh?"

"Yeah, I'm going to see my father," Sydney admitted shyly as she moved forward with the line.

"True, that's nice. Sometimes I go see my *papi* on Thursdays with my sister and little brothers. But Tuesday trips are strictly for my *papi chulo*, if you know what I mean," she giggled.

Sydney smiled and nodded. "I'm Sydney," she offered, feeling like they should probably exchange names since the two had already shared such personal details.

"My name is Consuela, but everybody calls me Connie," the girl responded as she pulled out her twenty and turned to hand it to the man. "Morning, Bob, how you feeling?"

"One day at a time," he responded automatically as he handed her a ticket and indicated that she could board the already full van.

"Sir, about how long is the drive," Sydney asked politely as she handed over her crisp twenty-dollar bill.

Realizing he had a new passenger on board, Bob paused to look up at Sydney. "You got about four hours depending on the traffic. Normally, it ain't too bad," he responded as he handed her a ticket. "We make one bathroom break each way, and any snacks you eat, you'd better clean up. This is your receipt and return ticket. Don't lose it or you're not getting back on the van to come home."

"Understood," Sydney replied as she tightened her grip on the small piece of paper. Bob finally gave her a head nod and Sydney stepped up into the van.

An unexpected bump in the road jolted Sydney awake. Momentarily disoriented, she looked confusedly at the van full of women and children surrounding her. "You was sleep a long time, ma," Connie said as the distinctive sound of Shakira's voice blared from the white earbuds she pulled out of her ears. "No worries, we 'bout to be there anyway."

"Hmm," was all Sydney could muster as she looked down at the square face of her Cartier watch. It was already after ten o'clock. She took a swig of the bottle of water she bought when they stopped at the gas station a couple of hours back to soothe her dry mouth and stared out the window as they hurtled down I-75. Everything looked so foreign; she'd never been out this deep in Georgia before.

"It's going to be a nice day," Connie commented as she looked over Sydney's shoulder out the window. Her breath smelled like cinnamon candy.

"Yeah, looks that way," Sydney replied, wishing she'd remembered to buy some gum. She turned to face her new acquaintance. "Do you have an extra piece of gum," she asked as Connie popped another small bubble.

"Umm-hmm," Connie replied as she started digging through her cheap-looking Louis Vuitton knockoff. "I always carry at least two packs with me at all times. Chewing gum helps relax my nerves."

"Thanks," Sydney said gratefully as Connie finally handed her a small square of original-flavored Trident.

"De nada," Connie replied as the van slowed down to exit on a sharp U-turn ramp.

Sydney's stomach tightened as she saw the small sign on the side of the road that read: CENTRAL STATE PRISON/ 5 MILES. She was both excited and extremely nervous to see Dice. While she really missed him, she also had a lot of unanswered questions about his connection to Jermaine's brother, Rodney, her newly discovered Uncle Larry, Keisha, and, of course, Altimus. She just hoped that their allotted fifty-five minutes of visitation time was enough to cover everything.

Connie pulled out a small leopard-print compact and applied her makeup. First, there was the heavy black eyeliner and mascara for her almond-shaped eyes. Then, she finished off with powder and a cherry-red gloss. Fluffing her hair out with her hands, she turned to Sydney. "It's better to do this now 'cause, trust me, you don't want to use their bathrooms," she warned ominously. Sydney absentmindedly ran a hand over her curly mane as she continued to watch Connie pull herself together. She looked at her watch; the Brookhaven student body would be moving to third period by now. Sydney pulled out her iPhone and sent a text to her sister.

Just wanted to let you know I'm good/ Almost there.

Again the van started to slow down for a sharp curve; Sydney squeezed her iPhone, anxious. This time they were entering the prison parking lot. After circling the half-empty lot, the van finally pulled into a space away from the smatter of cars already parked there.

"Okay y'all," Bob announced as soon as he threw the van's gear in park and it jerked to a complete stop. "We're pulling up outta here at eleven-fifteen with or without you. So don't be lagging behind or lose your ticket, 'cause your behind will get left." And with what he considered a fair warning administered, he jumped out to open the door and let the ladies loose.

Sydney followed Connie out of the van. As they started walking toward the huge iron gate where the first entrance was located, Sydney noticed that most of the women on the van had applied fresh coats of makeup. Buckling to the peer pressure, she grabbed her new favorite pink lip gloss, from Estee Lauder's Tender Lip Balm line, out of the side pocket of her purse and reapplied. Her iPhone vibrated; it was an incoming message from Lauren. Be careful slumming with the convicts/I got you covered — they don't suspect a thing.

Cool, Sydney wrote back quickly, before turning her attention back to Connie.

"Okay, so once we pass this guy here, we'll be brought into the locker room," stated Connie knowledgably. "You have to put all your stuff except for your driver's license into one of the lockers. After that, we'll sign in and go wait for them to meet us in the visitation room. Takes about fifteen minutes depending on the mood of the admitting officer. God forbid they're in a bad mood, 'cause then we're screwed. They'll take forever filling out the paperwork and checking IDs. Which cuts down on our visiting time. So fingers crossed, today will be a good day and we can get admitted in about fifteen minutes or so."

"Sounds simple . . ." Sydney replied, raising her two crossed fingers.

"Pretty much. As long as you have your ID and the person you're here to visit ain't got in no trouble and thrown in the hole over the last week, you're golden," Connie replied with a smile and final crack of gum.

"When they said I had a visitor, I was so sure it was a mistake, I almost didn't come out," Dice admitted when he finally released Sydney from his tight embrace. Tears shined in the corner of his eyes. "How ya doing, Ladybug?"

"I miss you, Dad," Sydney replied softly, still holding Dice's hand tightly as the two finally took a seat on one of the many steel benches in the large room that might've resembled a small cafeteria in another setting.

"I miss you more, sweetie," Dice responded sincerely. "What's going on? Is Lauren okay? I'm almost scared to ask what brought you up here."

Sydney took a deep breath and exhaled slowly. A million and one thoughts raced through her head. "Lauren is fine. But, no, everything is not okay."

Dice looked into his elder daughter's eyes. "You know about Altimus don't you," he stated flatly.

"Yeah, I do," Sydney responded. "I know about Altimus and I know about Mom —"

"What do you know about your mother," Dice cut her off sharply.

"I know that she knows who Altimus really is and she's okay with it. More important, I know that she doesn't care if you're innocent or not. All she wants to do is be with a man who'll provide a certain lifestyle for her even if it means killing somebody!"

"Shh, Sydney, lower your voice," Dice pleaded, checking to see if anyone was listening in on their conversation.

"I don't care, it's the truth," Sydney insisted, getting worked up. "And I don't want my *real* father sitting in a damn jail cell one minute longer if that man is the one responsible for what happened to Rodney!"

"Sydney, close your mouth and listen to me," Dice continued gruffly, trying to get Sydney to calm down without drawing attention to themselves among all the groups of inmates and their visitors. "You don't understand everything that you're dealing with right now. You could be in a lot of trouble if Altimus knows that you know who he is."

"I know. That's why I want to go to the police," Sydney started.

"For what?" her father asked sarcastically. "Don't you think Altimus has that covered already? Come on, Ladybug, you're smarter than that."

For the first time in the conversation Sydney hesitated. "So then what, you're just going to go back to jail? I'm going to lose you all over?"

"No, I didn't say that," Dice continued slowly. "Just like your stepfather, I've got people on the streets that have always been loyal to me. And we're working on clearing up this whole Rodney situation in a way that I can be released, and Altimus can be squared away as well. But it's not going to happen overnight."

"Who are these people," Sydney asked. "Speaking of unknown people, who the hell is Uncle Larry? You know he approached Lauren and allegedly saved her from getting an ass beating in the West End."

"Your Uncle Larry is one of the good guys. But can you please tell me why Lauren was in the West End?" Dice asked wearily as he rubbed his temples. Suddenly, he seemed a lot older than thirty-nine.

"Running behind Rodney's brother, Jermaine. You know that's her boyfriend," Sydney replied simply. "And Altimus has him on the run."

"Life is crazy," Dice said, rubbing his temples. "Damn, that kid shouldn't be mixed up in all of this; he's a good kid. Now, his brother, Rodney . . ."

"Can you please explain your connection to Rodney, Dad? 'Cause why would the cops think you killed him?"

"I met Rodney when I was locked up. We were cellmates for about six months before he got transferred out." Dice gently tugged at his right earlobe. According to him, Altimus asked him to do a job many years back when he was a new jack to prove his loyalty to the life."

"A job? What kind of job?"

"According to Rodney, Altimus asked him to set some poor sucker up in a gun-smuggling sting operation that one of the boys from the East Side tipped us off about. . . ."

Sydney gasped. "Rodney is the one that set you up?"

"It looks that way," Dice said with a resigned sigh.

"So why didn't you go to the cops? Why didn't Rodney tell the cops that you were the wrong man?"

"And spend an additional twelve years behind bars?

Rodney had fourteen months and I was about to be released in another year when this happened. It didn't make sense to start snitching. Besides, I could tell that behind that big mouth, Rodney was a good kid at heart. He just got caught up in Altimus's tangled web." Sydney put her head in her hands and began to cry silently in disbelief. How was she going to tell Lauren that her boyfriend's brother was the very person that sent their father to jail? And their stepfather requested he do it? "So instead of ratting, Rodney vowed to expose Altimus's ways to the streets," Dice continued softly.

"How would that do anything but piss Altimus off and obviously get him killed?" Sydney asked as she struggled to understand this lifestyle that was so foreign to her, yet seemed to have so many deep connections to her.

"If dudes on the street were to find out that Altimus set up his partner, they'd lose all respect and loyalty to him. Without respect and loyalty, Altimus will be completely powerless."

"So he killed him," Sydney whispered, looking up with a tear-stained face. Dice simply shrugged and looked at the shiny linoleum floor he'd been assigned to mop earlier in the morning.

"All right, peoples, start to wrap it up. You got fifteen minutes," one of the correction officers who periodically walked through the huddles of people announced.

"Aww, man, we just got here," an inmate complained from across the room.

"Shut it up or you're going to be heading the hell outta here and into the hole, Rodriguez," the officer responded menacingly. Sydney shuddered at his tone of voice.

"Promise me you'll stay out of your mother and Altimus's way," Dice said as he gently tucked a flyaway curl behind Sydney's left ear. "Okay, Ladybug?"

Across the room, Sydney spotted Connie and what could only be her *papi chulo* in a deep embrace. "Oh, Dad, this is so bad. I- I- I-" Sydney stammered.

"I nothing, Sydney. You have to trust me," Dice continued. "I need you to be strong and hold it down. There's no time for tears. If we're going to win, you have to stop being emotional and think strategically. I need you to be a soldier. Do you think you can you handle that?"

Sydney wiped her face with the back of her hand and straightened up. " I don't think, I know."

18
LAUREN

Lauren saw the teacher's mouth moving, but really, she couldn't comprehend a word she was saying, and that wasn't just because she hadn't done any of the assigned reading. Edward P. Jones's *The Known World* was Ms. Girard's latest obsession, and she'd been yapping about it for the past two days — something about African-American slave owners and death and black/white relationships in the South and God knows what else. Lauren had already put Donald on notice that it would be his job to read that mess and explain the plot details over coffee sometime this week; she was too distracted to glom into all of that ancient history. Luckily, boyfriend was officially obsessed with ole Eddie P., his stories, and particularly his loner lifestyle. Lauren couldn't begin to understand why, but whatever. This afternoon, she had more important things to consider, like, whether her sister actually made it to the prison, if they performed a cavity search on her to check for drugs and contraband like they do in all the cable prison shows, or whether she was dead in a ditch on the side of the road in East Bumblefreak, Georgia. And, of course, where her Jermaine was.

He'd called her repeatedly over the past few days, imploring her to "hit me back when you get this," and "just be careful — watch your back," and swearing that he was "maintaining," but that he needed to hear her voice to assure himself that "everything's everything." "It's going to be all right, baby," he'd said in his last message, left late Monday night. "I love you."

As much as she wanted to, Lauren didn't answer the phone and refused to call him back — confident that doing so would lead Altimus straight to him. Maybe she'd watched one too many *Law & Order* episodes, but didn't she see somewhere that the police could trace your whereabouts by tracking the sound waves from your phone? It was like a low-tech GPS, or something — at least that's what Lauren had convinced herself of, which is why she hadn't answered.

This was tearing her apart. But at least she knew that as long as the phone rang, Jermaine was all right, which is why it never left her side. (Well, that, and because she was scared that Keisha, Altimus, or their dedicated snoop would find it if she didn't keep it with her at all times. They'd gone through practically every inch of the girls' belongings, in front of them, and, for sure, when they weren't around. So as long as they didn't frisk her, Lauren thought it would be best to keep the phone on her person at all times.

"Excuse me, Ms. Girard, but I really need to go to the nurse's office," Dara said loudly, interrupting Lauren's thoughts. "I'm not feeling well — a little nauseous."

"A little, huh?" Lauren sneered. A few of their classmates smirked; nobody was feeling Dara's baby drama — thought it was quite tacky, actually. But mostly, they expected such hood behavior from Dara, considering she was the scholarship kid of a woman who made her living off the child-support checks. Obviously, her mama taught her well.

Dara whipped her head around and rolled her eyes at Lauren, and then subtly rubbed her belly and smirked. "Not sure what it is, but it certainly could have something to do with the company I'm forced to keep," she said as she moved her hand and turned her head back in the direction of the teacher, but clearly directed her words to Lauren.

"Okay, bring me your notebook — I'll sign you out," Ms. Girard said, ignoring the catfight and waving Dara to the front. "Maybe the lunchroom will have some crackers and ginger ale on hand for you." Dara, all 110 pounds of her, slowly wobbled up to the desk and shifted from foot to foot waiting for the teacher to scribble her name in the appointment book that doubled as a student hallway pass.

Ms. Girard's eyes lingered on Dara's belly; she shook her head and handed the appointment book back to her. "Don't forget we'll be having an in-class essay on the first five chapters this Thursday — study up," Ms. Girard mumbled.

"Yes, ma'am, I'll do my best," Dara said, making a beeline for the door.

And just then, Lauren's oversized Prada saddlebag began to vibrate. Jermaine. Lauren furrowed her eyes and stared at her bag. There were still two more periods left until school ended. Like clockwork, Jermaine always called after school was over, no doubt because he knew she'd be more likely to pick up without repercussions (calling, receiving calls, and texting were strictly forbidden at Brookhaven, and violators were subject to a two-hour detention — a penalty Lauren had paid one too many times). So what was he doing calling her now?

The phone finally stopped vibrating but then started back almost immediately, and then again, and again. Lauren's eyes darted back and forth between her TAG and her purse; with each vibration, her heart beat faster and faster still. It had to be some kind of emergency — otherwise, why would he keep dialing? She put her purse on her lap and held it close to her stomach.

Three more minutes listening to Ms. Girard's drivel, and she was going to find out.

* * *

"About practice today — I think we should do it outside so the new girls get used to cheering in the cold . . ." began Elizabeth, Lauren's new number two on the squad since Dara departed, jumping up in Lauren's face as soon as the bell rang.

"Yeah, listen, I make the decisions about practice," Lauren said, distracted. She was fighting her way through the rush of students making the mad in-between class dash to their lockers before the late bell rang; she needed to get to the bathroom, pronto.

"But it's supposed to be really cold this Friday, and the girls aren't really acting like they're up for —"

"Elizabeth? Seriously? I don't have time for this," Lauren said, pushing the door to the girls' bathroom open. She let it swing in Elizabeth's face and secretly hoped that it bumped her just a little — payback for putting her business with Jermaine on blast on YRT (she knew it was her — incurable gossip that she was).

Immediately, Lauren started digging for the phone, her fingers rushing over her compact, various M.A.C. Lipglass containers, a pack of Orbit gum, Breathsavers, notebooks, bobby pins, her wallet, a tube of L'Occitaine shea butter hand cream, a bottle of Dasani water she'd been sipping since that morning — there. Got it. Just as her fingers touched the phone, it vibrated again. She snatched it out of her purse and rushed into the handicapped stall at the end of the bathroom, where she'd have room to spread out and a little more privacy. She flipped open the cell, fully expecting to see "My Boo" flashing across the screen.

But it wasn't Jermaine.

It was her home number.

Lauren dropped the phone like it was as hot as fire and watched in terror as it slid across the tiled floor. It spun to a stop next to the garbage can, making a loud crashing sound that echoed off the walls of the spacious bathroom. The phone's vibration made the small metal can rattle. Lauren's hands were at her mouth — trembling.

Someone at the Duke Estate was calling her on Jermaine's phone.

Too afraid to answer, Lauren stood there and watched the phone rattle on and on, until, finally, it came to a rest. The sound of the bell made Lauren practically jump out of her skin. Quickly, she reached down and picked up the phone, pondering whether she should trash it, or use it to call Sydney to let her know not to bother coming back home, or use it to call 911 and report that Jermaine might be somewhere hurt, or worse.

Again, the phone vibrated.

Again, it was home.

Again, Lauren trembled, unsure of what to do.

Again, the phone went to voice mail.

It rang, again.

But this time, it wasn't home. It was a familiar 678 area code — Jermaine's house. Lauren swiped at the tears running down her face and smiled. He had to be okay, right? He was calling on the phone from his house. Somehow, Altimus or Keisha found his cell phone, but they didn't find him. Maybe, just maybe, they didn't find him.

"Hello? Jermaine?" Lauren whispered.

"No, this ain't Jermaine," the voice said shakily. There were muffled sobs and sniffles. It was a woman. "This is his mother. Who is this?"

"It's . . . this is . . . this is Lauren," Lauren said, returning her sobs with her own.

"Lauren? Lauren who?"

"Duke, ma'am," Lauren said. "I'm Lauren Duke."

"Duke?" she spit. "Duke? You mean Jermaine was still calling you even with all that's going on? Even though I told him to leave you alone?"

"What do you mean was?" Lauren interrupted.

"I should have known, Lord, have mercy, I should have known. I found the phone bills in his room — got this number all over them. I didn't know he even had this little phone. Of all the people, why you?"

"What do you mean 'was'?" Lauren repeated. "You said, 'was' calling me. Where is Jermaine? Is he there with you?"

"I was hoping whoever this phone number belonged to would be able to tell me. I haven't seen my son since yesterday morning. He wasn't where he was supposed to be today. Now, where is my child?" Eugenia Watson demanded.

"I . . . I . . . I don't know, Mrs. Watson," Lauren insisted, crying harder still. "I just don't know."

Lauren and Sydney sat in silence in the back of the massive SUV, staring at the back of the seats, each one lost in her own thoughts and fears. Lauren could hear each and every deep breath Sydney inhaled and exhaled. She imagined that this is what it must feel like to walk that long, lonely stretch to the executioner's room. And how it must feel to plan a funeral for someone you love — perhaps even your own.

Her heart beat faster with every street turn.

And faster still when Caesar pulled into the long, circular driveway, past the branchless crate myrtles and the prized purple hydrangea and the magnolias and encore azaleas and outstanding oaks and the fountain.

When they turned their eyes toward the front entrance to the Duke estate, both of their hearts seemingly stopped beating altogether.

Altimus and Keisha stood tall, arms folded, eyes deliberate.

Waiting.

Acknowledgments

DENENE

In the 12 books I've authored or co-authored, I've told the people who matter most to me how much they inspire my love of writing; they continue to do so, and I thank them every day for that. But this time around, I want to reserve my prettiest words for the two people who played a much larger role in my becoming a successful writer than they will ever know — they are my 11th-grade honors English teacher and my high school guidance counselor. The teacher told me my writing sucked; the guidance counselor insisted that I, an A-student/VP student council rep/school radio show host, was unqualified to win a much-needed college scholarship and that I should "try" to get into the community school down the block from my house. A hearty "thanks" to you both for the rousing support; your doubt in my abilities — and me — made me step up my game and become more successful than either of you suspected this little black girl could ever be. Good looking out.

For my co-author, Mitzi, the funniest, most energetic, tell-it-like-it-is girl I know: I tell you often that you need medication and Jesus, but I don't really mean it. I love you *exactly* the way you are (and I don't think pills or the Lord would help anyway). No girl could ask for a better late-night-gossiping/giggle-inducing/Crunktastical.blogspot-loving/fashion-advice-having/road dog/partner-in-crime than you.

For my agent, Victoria: All the way, baby! Attica!

And for the good folks at Scholastic, especially Andrea Davis Pinkney, Aimee Friedman, Abigail McAden, Jennifer Sanger, and Samantha Wolfert: Thank you for seeing the vision, appreciating the words, and making "Hotlanta" sizzle!

And lastly, my mom, Bettye Millner, and my sweet niece, Zenzele Thornton — two angels who make a home in Heaven, but always have a place in my heart.

MITZI

As a daughter of Yemaya, I am always grateful for the abundant blessings and opportunities that orisha brings into my life.

I would like to thank all of the family and friends who surround me with love and light.

Special acknowledgements are due to:

My mom, Elsa Miller a.k.a E-Dub; the rock star I've been emulating my whole life.

My dad, Guillermo Miller; who still allows me to be the Queen of Hartswood Rd.

My sister, Melissa; for always helping me find my keys and courage.

My Tia Puchi; your resiliency continues to amaze.

My Uncle Rick; may the good times in your life continue to roll.

My 'favoritest' cousin Roy & the boys; my personal militia of gentlemen.

My godfather and his partner in crime; Carlos and Israel; a million thank you's.

My godson, JJ; the apple of my eye.

My second family, Mommy Sally, Reginald, Chelsea, Pam, Maggie, Velma, Mary and all the kids; who still love me even though I used to pee in my pants.

My lifesaver, Maureen Davis; the best transplant coordinator an incorrigible noncompliant patient could ask for.

My mentors, Dr. Mitchell, Joyce and ABM; effortlessly leading by example.

The ladies on my short list — Mali, Joan, Shayla, Carmen, Carla, Kenya, Lisa, Daina, Toya, Juleyka, and Rhea.

The NYC clique — Sharae, Karina, Nicole, Bettina, KD, Takara, Christina, Melissa, Crystal, Geoff, Djena, Aliah, Tricia, Helen, Kiss, Monique, Daria, and K-Borders.

My FAMU family — Dara, Satonja, Nikki, Anika, and Kia.

My writing partner in crime (and real life superhero) — Tracee, a.k.a Trace-ba-Dace.

The fantastic men who inspire me to grind harder — Frank, Anthony, Dean, Malcolm Datwon, Wes, Ilan, Lo, XL, Musa, and K-Hova.

Thank you to the phenomenal Scholastic team. Andrea, Aimee, Abigail, Samantha, and Jennifer. You ladies have gone absolutely above and beyond to make this series a success. It is a pleasure working with you.

To Victoria Sanders, thank you for making sure all the i's are dotted and t's are crossed.

To my co-author, Denene; it's so hard to believe that something this fun is considered work. Thank you for the countless hours of laughter and tomfoolery. I rest easier at night knowing that in case of emergency you possess the knowledge to spring me out of the county clink.

Last but not least, my only child, Drama; because I know you understand English and despite your stinky farts and doggie breath, I honestly don't know what I would do without you by my side.

STAY ON TOP OF THE DRAMA.
TAKE A SNEAK PEEK AT

WHAT GOES AROUND
A HOTLANTA NOVEL

by Denene Milner and Mitzi Miller

SYDNEY

"Oh, so you think you cute," sneered the twins' evil-looking mother, Keisha Duke, from the open doorway as Sydney stood by her desk, disconnecting her iPhone from the charger.

Refusing to make eye contact, Sydney simply looked down and shrugged her shoulders. "I don't know what you're talking about."

"You don't know what I'm talking about?" questioned Keisha as she stepped into Sydney's bedroom and closed the door firmly behind her. "Well, please let me break it down for you. I'm talking about that little boy sitting in my living room, waiting on you. Because for some reason, he thinks that the two of you are going on a date."

"His name is Jason," Sydney retorted as she turned away from her mother to throw her wallet and cell into the silver Balenciaga bag sitting on her bed. "And for your information, we *are* going out on a date."

"Is that so? 'Cause it seems to me, I already done told you how I felt about that situation months ago. But maybe I wasn't clear enough," Keisha sneered. "Here's the deal, princess—your father and I donated a lot of damn money to Councilwoman Greene's campaign. Not just this past election or even the last; I'm talking on a continuous basis. Donation, dinners, gifts—you name it, we gave it. And it all equals way too much for you to be 'going out' with someone other than her beloved only son."

"Excuse me?"

"Oh, no, you heard me correctly," Keisha continued as she walked up directly behind her daughter. "Every hand greases the wheel. The security and longevity of our family business depends on making the right connections. And be clear, your little star quarterback sitting in my living room looking crazy ain't part of the program. So you can play dumb as long as you like, but at the end of the day, a winning pass ain't gonna save none of our asses from jail!"

Sydney turned around slowly and looked at her mother from head to toe with newfound contempt. "You know what? I really don't care how much money you and my *step*father donated to Marcus's mom's campaign. Everything done in the dark eventually comes to light. And there's no amount of money or greasing palms that's going to save either of you. And remember, I said you, not me!"

"Oh, please, who the hell are you kidding?" Keisha laughed. "You *are* me, little girl!"

"No, I'm not," Sydney retorted angrily.

"Wow, I always thought you were the smart one," Keisha mused nastily.

"Whatever, mother. You may be able to dictate what goes on in this house but you can't tell me who to be in a relationship with. And I'm certainly not about to stay with Marcus to help save you when you wouldn't even stay in your marriage to help save my father!" Sydney grabbed her bag, stepped around her mother, and headed for the door.

Jason waited nervously on the edge of the living room couch, where Sydney's mother had left him waiting. Looking at his watch, he increasingly regretted with each passing second his decision to arrive five minutes early. Suddenly, the door connected to the kitchen swung open and Altimus's figure filled the entire frame.

"Good evening, Mr. Duke," Jason said as he jumped up to offer his hand.

"I don't believe we've met," Altimus replied, gruffly choosing to dismiss both Jason's greeting and outstretched hand.

"Um, no we haven't. I mean, not formally," Jason replied nervously. "My name is Jason. Jason Darden. I'm a friend of Sydney's from Brookhaven. I was at the holiday party at Lake Lanier. . . ."

"I see," Altimus countered coolly. "Well, there was a lot going on that evening. You'll forgive me for not remembering you. In my line of work, I rarely forget a face."

"Oh, it's okay," Jason interjected, secretly relieved that Mr. Duke didn't recognize him from the tangle of bodies involved in the melee at Sydney's holiday-party brawl.

"Yet, I've never seen you around here before."

"Well, yeah. Sydney and I just started hanging out recently. I'm not from here. . . ."

"And just where would you be from, Jason?"

"Well, my folks moved down here about two years ago from New York City. So I just recently started going to school with Syd . . . I mean Sydney," Jason continued nervously.

"I see. And what brought your parents down to Atlanta?" Altimus asked, continuing his poker-faced interrogation without so much as a blink of an eye.

"Well, actually *I* did," Jason explained as he ran his sweaty palms down the front of his dark indigo Evisu jeans. "I wanted to play football in an area where I could easily get noticed by the college scouts, and my coach recommended the Atlanta area—"

"But Brookhaven doesn't win games." Altimus cut him off sharply with a raised eyebrow.

"This is true," Jason concurred. "But there was no way my parents were going to let me go to a school that didn't have a strong academic program, and let's just say Brookhaven has the best reputation by far. So my hope is that over the next year, I can help turn the football program around."

"Hmm, I'd have to agree with your parents. Reputation is very important," Altimus said simply. "Sydney has worked very hard to build and maintain her outstanding reputation both academically *and* socially."

Jason cleared his throat and shifted from one foot to the other. "Sydney's definitely a great person. I, uh, I'm looking forward to getting to know her," he started awkwardly.

"So it goes without saying that both Mrs. Duke and I have great expectations for our daughter. None of which will be achieved if she becomes sidetracked."

"Yes, sir."

"And while neither her mother nor myself would ever propose to choose who our daughter spends her time with," Altimus continued, "I'm sure you can understand *my* concern after years of walking into this room and greeting the Honorable Councilwoman Greene's son, Marcus. You do know Marcus Greene don't you?"

"Yeah, I know him." Jason bristled slightly at the mention of Sydney's ex-boyfriend.

"Well, then, I'm sure you can understand how I might feel about finding you here now," Altimus continued unapologetically.

"Understood," Jason responded from between clenched teeth.

"As long as we're clear," Altimus concluded just as Sydney bounded down the staircase into the living room. She paused at the end of the staircase for effect. Altimus reflexively clenched his teeth.

"Hey, J," Sydney said, rewarding Jason with a huge smile as she unknowingly interrupted the tense moment.

"Hey, Sydney. You look nice," Jason responded, grateful for the opportunity to escape from Altimus's thinly veiled scare tactics.

"Thanks. So do you." Sydney paused for a moment to take in Jason's jeans, buttoned-up shirt, and fresh pair of Nike Air Force Ones. Even though the jeans were much baggier than his infamous uniform pants, Jason still looked really good.

"Altimus, did you meet my friend Jason?" Sydney inquired, oblivious to the tension in the room.

"Yes, I did," Altimus responded. "As a matter of fact, Jason and I were talking about future prospects when you came down."

"Of what? The Brookhaven team?" Sydney asked, looking quizzically at Jason for a clue to what her stepfather was talking about.

"Something like that," Jason answered vaguely with a slight smile Sydney couldn't figure out. "You ready to go?" he asked.

"Yeah, my shoes are at the door," Sydney answered as she headed to the front door in search of her black-and-silver Gucci ballet flats.

"Cool," Jason said. "It was nice to meet you, Mr. Duke," Jason said, offering his hand again.

"I'm sure," Altimus responded, and walked away.

LAUREN

Lauren practically tiptoed to the tiny refrigerator tucked in the corner of the hot pink Duke cheerleading clubhouse lounge and opened it as gingerly as possible. But still, the sound of her Nikes squeaking across the pristine white tile and the shifting of the water bottles in the refrigerator door made her headache pound even harder. She'd been fighting the migraine all day, but four bathroom passes, two Alleve, a cup of herbal tea, and a visit to the nurse's office later, and Lauren was still rubbing her temples and sending up silent prayers to God begging him to "take the pain away, so I can show these wannabes how a true dance captain gets down." Under normal circumstances, she would have sent a pleading text to her mom, imploring her to put in a call to the school nurse; an early release, an afternoon nap, and an episode or two of *Law & Order: SVU* would have been fitting recompense for the trauma her body was going through, and Keisha, God bless her soul, would have been too preoccupied with her Wednesday afternoon nail salon visit to care if Lauren dipped out of a couple of classes. But there was no time for the zone-out. Word on the curb was that a sophomore on the basketball dance squad was gunning for Lauren's No. 1 spot, and migraine be damned if she was going to just let somebody come in and steal her head-cheerleader-in-charge title. About this much Lauren was clear: Lauren Duke wasn't about to go down without a fight.

She reached into the refrigerator and grabbed the Tupperware container full of cucumber slices she kept stashed for occasions such as these. A twenty-minute power nap in the plush recliner with the cucumber slices on her eyes would work wonders on her headache and surely take away the puffiness that had settled just under her lower eyelids; she'd wake up refreshed and ready to show those heiffas just why she was, and needed to remain, the dance squad captain.

Lauren settled into the recliner and set her iPhone alarm for 3:20 P.M.; that would give her about ten minutes after she awakened to change into her gear and go over the new steps in her head before the rest of the team arrived at the locker room to get ready for practice. But no sooner had she placed the soothing cucumbers on her eyes and rested her head on her special pillow than she heard a stall door in the bathroom slam shut.

"Who's that?" Lauren said, bolting upright. The cucumbers tumbled between the chair's arm and seat cushion.

There was no answer.

To Do List: Read all the Point books!

By Aimee Friedman

- ❑ South Beach
- ❑ French Kiss
- ❑ Hollywood Hills
- ❑ The Year My Sister Got Lucky

❑ **Airhead** by Meg Cabot

❑ **Suite Scarlett** by Maureen Johnson

❑ **Love in the Corner Pocket** by Marlene Perez

❑ **This Book Isn't Fat, It's Fabulous** by Nina Beck

Hotlanta series by Denene Millner and Mitzi Miller

- ❑ Hotlanta
- ❑ If Only You Knew

❑ **Top 8** by Katie Finn

❑ **Popular Vote** by Micol Ostow

By Pamela Wells

- ❑ The Heartbreakers
- ❑ The Crushes

Summer Boys series by Hailey Abbott

- ❑ Summer Boys
- ❑ Next Summer
- ❑ After Summer
- ❑ Last Summer

❑ **Orange Is the New Pink** by Nina Malkin

Making a Splash series by Jade Parker

- ❑ Robyn
- ❑ Caitlin
- ❑ Whitney